ALSO BY KIRBY LARSON

Novels

Dear America: The Fences Between Us

The Friendship Doll

Hattie Big Sky

Hattie Ever After

Picture Books
with Mary Nethery

Nubs: The True Story of a Mutt, a Marine & a Miracle

*Two Bobbies: A True Story of Hurricane Katrina,
Friendship, and Survival*

DUKE

KIRBY LARSON

Scholastic Press / New York

Library of Congress Cataloging-in-Publication Data
Larson, Kirby.
Duke / Kirby Larson. — 1st ed.
p. cm.
Summary: In 1944 Hobie Hanson's father is flying B-24s in Europe, so Hobie decides to donate his beloved German shepherd, Duke, to Dogs for Defense in the hope that it will help end the war sooner — but when he learns that Duke is being trained for combat he is shocked, frightened, and determined to get his dog back.
ISBN 978-0-545-41637-5 (jacketed hardcover) 1. German shepherd dog — Juvenile fiction. 2. World War, 1939–1945 — United States — Juvenile fiction. 3. Dogs — War use — Juvenile fiction. 4. Human-animal relationships — Juvenile fiction. 5. United States — History — 1933–1945 — Juvenile fiction. [1. German shepherd dog — Fiction. 2. Dogs — Fiction. 3. Dogs — War use — Fiction. 4. World War, 1939–1945 — United States — Fiction. 5. Human-animal relationships — Fiction. 6. United States — History — 1933–1945 — Fiction.] I. Title.
PZ7.L32394Duk 2013
813.54 — dc23
2012046636

10 9 8 7 6 5 4 3 2 1   13 14 15 16 17

Printed in the U.S.A.   23
First edition, September 2013
The text type was set in Legacy Serif.
The display type was set in Champion and Didot.
Book design by Whitney Lyle

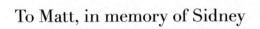

To Matt, in memory of Sidney

TABLE OF CONTENTS

CHAPTER ONE

Are YOU Doing Everything You Can?

Seattle, Washington
January 1, 1944

Hobie pushed harder against the bike pedals, harder against the cold wind scrubbing his face, as he followed the Adairs' Chrysler sedan. Duke loped along behind, pink tongue flapping. Even a smart dog like him would have no idea why they were out there, in the cold and wet, instead of home eating leftover Christmas cookies and reading the newest Hardy Boys mystery. Dogs didn't know what it was like to have best friends move away.

Legs burning, Hobie kept pumping. But he was no match for the last hill. The bike slowed, then clunked to a stop. He was out of steam. Dead in the water, as Dad might say. Panting, Hobie flung up his arm in one last good-bye wave. Mr. Adair answered by tapping the horn three times. As the sedan turned east, toward the highway to Portland, Scooter's head popped out the window. He yelled something, but the wind carried it away before it reached Hobie.

And then the car was gone.

Scooter was gone.

Duke brushed against Hobie's legs. "At least I've still got you," Hobie said, scratching the German shepherd behind the ears. "Right, boy?"

Hobie slid off his bike and began pushing it toward home, trying to catch his breath. The thought of school without Scooter made the pushing even harder. They'd been pals since first grade, when Scooter accidentally knocked out Hobie's front tooth with a tetherball. Luckily, it was a baby tooth. In the past four years, the only time Hobie had walked to school without Scooter was when the chicken pox was going around. He got itchy all over again thinking about how lonely Monday's walk was going to be.

Mom called Scooter a "pistol," but she would smile when she said it. Usually. That time with the whoopee cushion at her bridge club she didn't smile. But Hobie couldn't help chuckling even now, remembering the look on Mrs. Allen's face when she'd sat down.

The rain, coming down harder, soaked through Hobie's corduroy jacket to his T-shirt. After a block or so, he swung his leg over the bike and began pedaling again. Mrs. Lee was out, sweeping, even though her little grocery store was closed for the holiday. She waved as Hobie rode by.

He passed the playfield and then the school. He knew it would only make him feel worse, but Hobie rode to the far side of the building, peeking in Mrs. Thornton's fifth-grade classroom. The desk there, in the row farthest from the door, third back, would be empty on Monday. Hobie had helped Scooter clean it out, right before Christmas break. The schoolbooks went back in the supply cupboard, the pencils and erasers into Scooter's pencil pouch, and the comic books — the ones carefully hidden under a fan of old math work sheets — had been deftly tucked inside Scooter's jacket. Their teacher never saw a thing.

Mrs. Thornton must have come in over the vacation to put up that new poster on the wall behind her desk. A finger pointed out at Hobie over a caption that read, ARE YOU DOING ALL YOU CAN?

Hobie stepped away from the window, wiping moss from his hands. Everyone he knew was doing all they could. Dad had left Uncle Tryg in charge of the family fishing boat, the *Lily Bess*, to fly B-24s in Europe. Mom joined the Red Cross, and his little sister, June, was knitting socks for soldiers. Holey socks, sure, but she was only seven.

And now, the Navy needed Mr. Adair to work at the Portland shipyard. "Doncha know there's a war on?" Scooter had said, trying to make a joke when he told Hobie about the move. But neither of them had laughed.

Duke shook himself all over, spraying Hobie but good. "Okay, okay," he said. "We'll get going." As they turned away from the building, Hobie heard the *slap-slap-slap* of a basketball on pavement. Someone was shooting hoops in the covered area. He pedaled over to see who.

And when he saw, he backpedaled so fast he nearly ran into Duke.

Mitch Mitchell. Ever since he'd overheard Scooter and Hobie playing like they were Hop Harrigan and his sidekick, Tank Tinker, he hadn't missed a chance to take them down a notch, making fun of their "baby games." And that was one of the nicer things he said. Mitch could hit as hard with words as other guys could with fists.

Hobie gave a quiet whistle. He felt like an ant farm had burst open inside him. He needed to move, to shake everything off. "Beat you home!" he called to Duke, legs racing faster than his thoughts.

He was no longer plain old Hobie Hanson but Hop Harrigan, about to break the world's airspeed record. Hobie barreled down the sidewalk, popping over an exposed root before veering around an old lady in black lace-up shoes. She hollered at him as he flew by.

As their house came into sight, Duke launched into action. He stretched out his front legs, running in that funny rocking motion of his. Front legs, back legs. Front, back. Front, back. Well ahead of Hobie, he bounded up the porch steps and skidded against the door, panting.

Hobie was panting, too, as he rolled to a stop. Duke picked up one of his old tennis balls and trotted over, pushing his muzzle into Hobie's hand.

"What? I have to reward you for beating me?" Hobie buried his face in Duke's neck, breathing in his warm dustiness. If only Hobie could bottle this smell and keep it on his shelf, like Dad's Barbasol.

"Fetch!" Hobie cranked back his arm and chucked the ball. Again and again. No matter how far Hobie threw it, Duke snagged the ball before it hit the ground. It was like he had wings.

"The Army sure could use a dog like Duke." Mr. Gilbert stepped down from his front porch next door, pipe in hand. "My nephew sent his dog, and now he's guarding a munitions plant."

Hobie had heard about people doing that. There was even a song called "The K-9 Corps" playing on the radio lately: "From the kennels of the country, from the homes and firesides, too, we have joined the canine army, our nation's work to do." Hobie turned off the radio when it came on.

Duke nudged at his hands as if to say, "What are you waiting for? Throw the ball." Hobie patted him. Just because Duke *would* make a good guard dog didn't mean he *should* be one.

"We all have to do our part." Mr. Gilbert picked his newspaper up from the porch and tucked it under his arm.

That was easy for him to say. He had a dumb old cat. Not a dog.

"I think my mom needs me," Hobie said. "See you later."

He climbed the steps with legs as wobbly as if he'd ridden his bike up Mt. Rainier. So what if Mr. Gilbert's nephew donated his dog? Hobie was already doing his share. He couldn't even remember the last time he'd bought a comic book; he was spending all of his dimes on war stamps. K-9 Corps! Hobie yanked the door open, then let it slam shut.

"Your show's almost on!" June said. "Mommy said Kitty and I could listen, too." She held up the raggedy doll that she carried everywhere.

Hobie didn't really hear her; Mr. Gilbert's words got in the way.

A smooth radio announcer's voice filled the room, which was warm and damp from the heat of Mom's ironing. *"For 1944, let's all resolve: Eat a good breakfast and do a better job! And let crispy, toasty brown Grape-Nuts Flakes help make it easy for you."*

June danced Kitty on Hobie's head. "We like crispy, toasty brown Grape-Nuts Flakes, don't you?"

Hobie batted the doll away.

"Mommy!" June cried.

"Hobie, be kind to your sister." Mom licked her fingers, the iron hissing as she tested it. "Remember what your father said."

How could Hobie forget? "You're the captain of this family while I'm gone," Dad had said. "I'm counting on you to step up and do what needs to be done."

Hobie had stepped up. He walked June to and from school every single day. He rode his bike to Lee's Grocery whenever Mom needed something. He mowed the lawn all summer and raked leaves in the fall. But to Dad, being a captain was more than actions, it was attitude.

He took a deep breath. "Sorry, June."

"Kitty forgives you." June proved it by dancing the doll on Hobie's knee.

The announcer came back on again. *"Presenting Hop Harrigan — America's Ace of the Airways!"*

Hobie scooted closer to the radio. In yesterday's episode, Hop got amnesia after a fight with some rotten Nazi spies. He'd been so confused, he didn't even recognize his good old sidekick, Tank.

Duke rested his head on Hobie's leg as they all listened to the latest installment. Thankfully, Hop recovered in the nick of time, just as he was about to spill the location of the professor's secret laboratory.

"That was a swell one," June announced. "Kitty's favorite so far."

"Shh." Hobie held his finger up to his lips. "There's more."

"This is your announcer with an important message from Hop. In the radio audience today are twin brothers Mike and Spike Jankelson. These two young Americans have loaned their collie, Laddie, to Uncle Sam. Hop wants you listeners out there to know he sure is proud of these boys. And he wants to encourage every dog owner to consider following Spike and Mike's lead —"

Hobie snapped the radio off.

"The show's not over!" June fussed.

"Pretty much."

"I wanted to hear the whole thing."

Hobie made a face. "Tune in tomorrow," he said, mimicking the announcer.

June flounced out of the room, taking Kitty with her.

Mom set the iron down. She tipped her head toward the radio. "There are lots of ways to help. But you don't have to do them all." She winked. "I think that last rubber drive should've earned you a purple heart."

Hobie felt his face get hot, remembering. Scooter thought it was as funny as a Laurel and Hardy movie, but Hobie had nearly shriveled up like a slug when Mrs. Lee donated not one but two of her old girdles.

He leaned his chin against the kitchen table. "Why did Dad enlist?" His head bounced up and down as he talked.

Mom sat down next to him. "There's no one answer. Mostly, he felt he could do something, make a difference." She ruffled Hobie's hair. "You and your dad are like two peas in a pod." She bent over, kissed the top of his head, then went back to her ironing.

Hobie's head felt too heavy to lift off the table. He wasn't like his father at all. Dad was brave. He did things, even if they were hard. Like taking the

Lily Bess up to Alaska each summer. Or helping Uncle Tryg keep an eye on the Sasakis' house after they got sent to those camps. Or leaving his family to fight in a war.

Hobie wasn't anything like that.

Because, deep down, even though he knew it was the right thing, he didn't think he could ever give Duke to the Army.

CHAPTER TWO

No, Duke!

January 3, 1944

Duke began to whine the minute Hobie bent down to tie his PF Flyers. "I wish you could come, too." Hobie scratched behind Duke's ears. "How about if I make it up to you with a bike ride after school?"

Duke's answer was to shake himself from tip to tail.

"Don't forget it's Monday!" Mom called down the hall. "Stamp day."

Hobie reached for his piggy bank and jiggled out a dime to buy another stamp. So far, he'd pasted nine dollars and forty cents' worth of them in his Victory book. Every week, Mrs. Thornton told the class how proud she was of the way they were buying stamps in honor of their country. But Hobie wasn't buying them for his country. He was buying them for Dad and everything he was doing. Thinking about that made Hobie shake out a second dime to take to school.

Duke followed Hobie to the front door, looking as innocent as a baby lamb, but Hobie was wise to his tricks. The minute Hobie opened the front door, Duke would try to squeeze through. Hobie held up his palm, signaling for Duke to sit. "Stay," he added.

Duke sat. He stayed.

He whined.

"I don't see why Duke can't come with us." June buttoned up her coat. "He minds better than any of the boys in my class. Smells better, too."

"June Margaret!" Mom scolded. "Ladies do not say such things."

"It's true." June swung her book bag.

Hobie tucked his books under his arm. "Bye, Mom."

Even before the door closed behind them, Hobie heard Duke's nails scrabbling against the linoleum. A second later, Duke's black nose was pressed against the front room window, right next to the blue star service flag hanging there for Dad.

"Be good," Hobie called to him. "I'll be home soon."

"Miriam thinks Duke is smarter than Lassie,"

June said. "I said he's smarter than Lassie and Toto and Fala, all rolled into one."

"He is arf-fully smart," Hobie joked. He paused as they turned down the sidewalk, trying to forget that conversation with Mr. Gilbert.

June struck a he-man pose. "And I bet he's even braver than Rin Tin Tin." She tilted her head back and howled like a wolf.

Hobie didn't want to talk about Duke anymore. "You better practice your words," he said. "You don't want Miriam to win the spelling ribbon, do you?"

June stamped her foot. "No, I don't!" She hopped over a puddle and began reciting. She finished the last word on her weekly list as they arrived at school.

"B-e-a-r, bear." June clapped her hands. "There. I'm going to get one hundred percent on the test!"

"Well, I'm going to get two hundred percent!" Miriam marched up to June, her hands on her hips.

"Three hundred percent!" June stuck out her tongue for emphasis.

Hobie pointed to the first-grade classroom. "Don't be late."

The two spelling rivals jockeyed for position, each trying to beat the other inside.

Down the hall, Hobie started into his own classroom. Then he stopped. There was something new, and it wasn't just that poster.

Someone was sitting at Scooter's desk. A kid whose ears stuck out in a friendly way.

"Hey," said Hobie.

"Hey," said the kid.

The final bell rang.

Mrs. Thornton looked out at her students. "Catherine? Will you lead us in the pledge of allegiance?"

"All rise," Catherine commanded. She stood at the front of the room, towering over everyone, even Mitch Mitchell. "With liberty and justice for all," she finished up before the rest of the students.

"For all," echoed the class.

"Before we do our Victory stamps, I'd like to introduce you to someone." Mrs. Thornton waved the new boy to the front. "This is Max Klein."

Other teachers might tell the new kid to say something about himself, but Mrs. Thornton was nicer than that. She studied each row of students. "I know without asking that each and every one of you will make Max feel welcome." Was it his imagination, or did Mrs. Thornton's gaze linger a bit longer on Hobie than on anyone else? He sat up straighter.

Max took his seat again quickly and began tapping the heels of his shoes against the chair legs. With shoes being rationed along with so many other things, most everyone was crunched into sneakers or oxfords at least one size too small. Kicking your foot back into your heels eased the pinching. Hobie had figured that out, too.

"I know you young citizens are eager to buy your war stamps," said Mrs. Thornton. "Form a line behind Catherine."

When it was his turn, Hobie slid his two dimes across Mrs. Thornton's desk and she slid two stamps back. "I'm so proud of you. You're halfway to a war bond."

Hobie's cheeks didn't cool down until Mrs. Thornton announced that it was time for science. "Please take out your textbooks," she said.

Hobie pulled out his book, glancing toward the new kid. A Green Lantern comic peeked out from underneath a composition book in his desk. Hobie smiled.

Mrs. Thornton asked Catherine and Marty to pass out work sheets. "Do your best to fill in the answers on your own," she said. "We'll go over them together before recess."

Hobie wrote his name at the top of the work sheet. He could tell from the first question that he should have done his science reading over vacation. He filled in all the blanks he could, then looked around the room. Most everyone else was still scribbling away. He'd better look busy, too. He drew a doodle on the page, lightly. It looked sort of like a shield. Like the one Captain America used. He added a few more lines.

"You're a good artist," Max whispered.

"Thanks," Hobie whispered back; then he put his arm up to block his drawing. If Max could see, so could anyone. Like Mrs. Thornton.

Hobie hunched over, adding a big star right in the center of the shield. Now it was practically like the one in the comics.

"Is everyone just about finished?" asked Mrs. Thornton. A few kids groaned. "Okay," she said. "One more minute."

Hobie flashed the finished work of art at Max,

earning a thumbs-up. He admired it once more himself and then set to work with the eraser end of his pencil. Mrs. Thornton would never know.

"Let's begin with the first question." Their teacher clapped her hands for attention. "Do any of my young citizens know why we're being asked to save cooking fats?"

Mitch's hand flew up. "To make bombs to take out the Nazis!" he said. "Ka-pow!" He glared at Max.

"But how are they used in the bombs?" Mrs. Thornton pressed. "Can anyone be more specific?"

Hobie stared at her. Mom saved every bit of grease in a can on the back of the stove. When it was full, he would ride it over to the butcher's. But now he realized he had no idea why.

From the corner of his eye, Hobie saw a hand inch up.

"Max?" Mrs. Thornton flashed her Ginger Rogers smile in his direction.

"The military extracts glycerin from the fats," he said. "To make the explosives."

"Very good!" Mrs. Thornton looked like she could turn a cartwheel for joy.

"Ka-pow," said Catherine. She giggled.

"I knew that," Mitch grumbled.

"Max, I can tell you are going to be a wonderful addition to our classroom." Mrs. Thornton brushed the chalk from her hands. "And now, my young citizens, it's time for recess."

The cloakroom was a jumble of everyone getting into coats and jackets. Mitch jabbed his elbow into Max's rib cage.

"I didn't see you buy a stamp today," he said.

Catherine edged over to the boys. "Leave him alone."

"Are you on his side?" Mitch asked. "Maybe you both want Hitler to win the war."

Hobie's stomach knotted like wet rope. The kid hadn't even been here one day and Mitch was starting in on him. He knew he should do something, but what? Hobie wished he'd inherited more than a name from his fisherman grandfather. Along with their tobacco juice, the old guys down at the docks spat out story after story of Hobart Hanson's bravery. Grandfather Hanson hadn't been afraid of anything: not hard, slippery work on his purse seiner, or the dark and icy sea, or the storms that chewed up boats steered by lesser captains.

But then Grandfather had never met Mitch Mitchell.

"I'm American," Max said, his voice catching, just for a second.

Mitch scoffed. "With a name like Klein?"

Catherine grabbed a ball from the bin. "Come on, Max. Play wall ball with Hobie and me." She tapped Hobie on the arm. As if to say they were a team.

Was Catherine crazy? Going against Mitch like this? Well, she could get away with it. She was a girl.

"Uh, I was thinking of going to the library —" Hobie started.

"Bluck, bluck, bluck." Mitch flapped his arms at Hobie. Then he turned to Max. *"Heil,* Hitler." He saluted before running outside.

Max blinked behind his glasses. "You don't have to be nice to me," he said to Catherine.

"Nice?" asked Catherine. "I'm not being nice." The look she gave Hobie was sad. No, disappointed. "I'm going to clean your clock."

Max snorted. "I'd like to see you try."

They ran off, too, leaving Hobie alone in the cloakroom. Alone and wondering, once again, why he couldn't have inherited more than a name from his grandfather.

CHAPTER THREE

Duke to the Defense

Later that same day

June came running out of her classroom. "Look!" She waved her spelling test. "A gold star!" She twirled on tippy-toe. "I didn't miss a word." She spun around and around like the little ballerina in her music box.

"That's great." Hobie snagged her mid-twirl. "Don't you want to hurry home and tell Mom?"

"Okay!" She started to prance like a pony, which was also embarrassing, but at least she was moving toward home, not spinning in one spot.

Hobie glanced over his shoulder. Catherine was running to her mother's DeSoto. Other kids lined up for the bus. Hobie cocked his head a bit. He could almost hear Scooter, making that day's rule for the walk home. "We step on every crack," he might say. Or, "We've got to crow like roosters at the corners." Scooter's favorite game was "hit-o-heap." If either boy spotted a real junker car rattling down the street, he popped the other on the arm. Scooter was loaded with ideas. And Hobie was great at going along with them.

He took one last look around, to make sure that Scooter wasn't going to leap out from behind the building, howling like a hyena at the prank he'd played. But there was no Scooter. Hobie didn't see Max anywhere, either. Or, thank goodness, Mitch.

"I wrote a letter in school today," June announced.

"Which letter?" Hobie teased. "'E'? 'A'?"

June punched his arm. "A real letter," she said. "To Scooter. Do you want to hear it?"

"Sure," he said. Though he wasn't so sure.

June fished a piece of paper from her book bag. "'Dear Scooter,'" she read. "'I wish your father wasn't so good at building boats. Then you wouldn't have to move. I wish you were here even if you do pull on my pigtails. Love, June.'" June cocked her head. "Is that a good letter?"

"Yeah." Hobie cleared his throat. "Yeah. That's a real good letter."

She didn't mean to, but June made him feel even worse about the day. It wasn't just Mitch calling him chicken. What about that look Catherine had given him? She probably wouldn't choose him for her dodgeball team in PE anymore.

He picked up the pace. He wanted to get home. To Duke. At least he still had Duke.

And there he was, at the front door, barking and licking, the minute Hobie stepped through. Hobie gave him a big hug. "Hey, buddy. How are you?"

He changed into his dungarees and devoured a couple of Mom's special oatmeal cookies, warm from the oven. Duke got a couple of bites, too.

"Going out, Mom!" Hobie called.

Duke bounded after him, determination radiating to the very tips of his coat. He'd been left behind that morning. He was not going to be left behind again.

Hobie hopped on his Schwinn, and off they went. Duke grinned as he loped along, keeping pace while Hobie rode to the playfield.

"Watch this!" Hobie pushed back on the pedals to engage the coaster brakes. "I'm going in for a landing, just like Hop." The bike careened this way and that as Hobie executed his maneuvers.

"CX-4 calling the tower, CX-4 calling the tower!" That's what Hop Harrigan said at the start of each radio program. Hop was an ace pilot, like Dad, except *he* flew the experimental CX-4, and Dad flew a B-24 he'd named *Lily Bess, Too*.

Hobie's legs slowed as he thought of Dad. Every spring, since before Hobie was born, Dad and Uncle Tryg went up to Alaska to fish. For months at a time, it'd be just Hobie, June, and Mom. Like it was now.

What was different about now was that Dad was in a war. He had said piloting was piloting, whether you were steering a boat or a plane. But there weren't any Germans shooting at him when he was out on the *Lily Bess*. Lately, a day didn't go by without an article in the paper about a pilot having to bail out somewhere over Europe. Even aces like Dad. That worry wore away at Hobie like salt water on a wooden hull.

A sharp bark cut through Hobie's thoughts. Duke's squirrel bark. He charged around Hobie, zooming off across the playfield, intent on one thing. Catching a squirrel.

"Duke!" Hobie dropped his bike and ran after him, even though he knew it was hopeless. That dog could not resist squirrels. "Come!"

Hobie followed the barking to the woods at the edge of the field. "Duke! Here!" His only answer was a *rat-a-tat* of barks.

Duke would come back. When he was tired. Hobie decided he'd best go retrieve his bike.

It was gone. Hobie looked around. A man in an overcoat and fedora was walking a Doberman pinscher.

"Did you see a bike lying here?" Hobie asked.

The man gestured behind Hobie. There, rolling down the sidewalk, was Mitch Mitchell.

"Get off," Hobie hollered. "That's mine."

"Finders keepers." Mitch pedaled faster. Hobie picked up his pace. He snagged part of Mitch's jacket. The bike wobbled. Mitch shook him off.

"Give it back!" Hobie ran harder.

"When I feel like it," Mitch called over his shoulder. He bumped the bike over a tree root. "Ya-hoo!"

"Young man!" the Doberman's master called. "That's enough. You've had your fun."

"Yeah. Come back here," Hobie yelled.

"Come back?" Mitch repeated. "Okay." He wrenched the bike around sharply, legs pumping like pistons, and headed straight at Hobie.

Hobie jumped aside at the last minute, grabbing for the handlebars. He missed. As Mitch whizzed past, he kicked at Hobie's knee. Pain shot through Hobie's leg. He crumpled in a heap.

Then there was a blur of fur and Mitch was hollering, "Call him off! Call him off!"

The man with the Doberman came running.

Duke gripped Mitch's pant leg in his teeth. "Duke!" Hobie had never seen him do anything like this before. "No!"

A deep growl rumbled in Duke's chest. His ears perked to alert. As if he knew Hobie was in danger.

"That dog just about bit me!" Mitch tried to get off the bike. A difficult feat with his dungarees caught in a German shepherd vise. "You saw it, didn't you?" He turned to the man.

"Drop!" Hobie scrambled to his feet. "Duke. Drop!"

Duke let go of Mitch's pant leg. Mitch scrambled away.

"Down." Hobie gave the hand signal along with the command.

Duke obeyed. He went down. But his brown eyes stayed locked on his target. It was clear he

27

intended to protect Hobie from Mitch, no matter what.

The man picked up Hobie's bike. "It takes a special person to be able to train a strong animal like that." He wheeled the bike over to Hobie. "He's your dog, I assume?"

"Mutt is more like it," Mitch grumbled, brushing off his pants.

Hobie nodded, taking his bike from the man.

"My name's Rasmussen."

The man stuck out his hand and Hobie reached over the handlebars to shake, saying, "Hobie Hanson."

Mr. Rasmussen's Doberman sat quietly by his side. If you didn't know dogs, you'd think he was asleep with his eyes open. But the muscle twitching in his left shoulder signaled that the Dobie was ready for whatever command Mr. Rasmussen might give next.

"This is my dog, Ludwig." The dog's head cocked slightly at his name. "Well, he's my dog for a little while longer. He's shipping out soon. Going to work for Uncle Sam for the duration." Mr. Rasmussen fingered Ludwig's pointed ears. "I'm going to miss this big galoot." He pulled a handkerchief from his pocket and passed it over his eyes. "But I could hardly keep him back, not when he could save some brave soldier's life." He re-pocketed his handkerchief.

"My brother's in the Marines." Mitch took a hesitant step toward Ludwig. "They have a couple of messenger dogs in their unit."

"Go ahead, you can pet him. But let him smell you first." Mr. Rasmussen showed Mitch what to do. "Dogs are doing lots of important jobs for the war effort," he said. "Though most stay right here, guarding the coastline or plants like Boeing."

Mitch scratched under Ludwig's chin.

Hobie rolled his bike forward and back a few times. "I better get home," he said.

But Mr. Rasmussen kept talking, and it would be rude to leave. "In fact, I've become such a believer, I signed on to recruit other dogs." He tilted his hat back. "I don't suppose you'd consider lending your dog, there."

Hobie looked at Duke. "Well, I —"

Mitch scoffed. "Him? Do anything like that?" He tucked his hands in his armpits and flapped his arms.

Hobie wished Mitch would beat it.

"This is no easy decision," Mr. Rasmussen said. "Trust me, I know." He paused. "I thought long and hard about sending Ludwig."

Hobie's shoulders loosened a bit.

"But a dog like that" — Mr. Rasmussen inclined his head toward Duke — "already so well trained — well, he'd be like the prize in the Cracker Jack box for the Army."

The whole time Mr. Rasmussen had been talking, he'd been stroking Ludwig's head. You'd have to be blind not to see how much he cared about that dog. Almost as much as Hobie cared about Duke. It couldn't have been easy for him. Not one bit.

"I don't know," Hobie said. He did want to help. He did!

"Tell you what." Mr. Rasmussen pulled a business card from his pocket. "Think it over. This is my number. If you decide to donate Duke, give me a call. There's a train going out this weekend, and he and Ludwig could both be on it."

Hobie glanced at the card: OLIN RASMUSSEN, ASST. REGIONAL DIRECTOR, DOGS FOR DEFENSE, TELEPHONE: MELROSE 2-0585. He put the card in his jacket pocket.

"Bye, now, boys." Mr. Rasmussen walked on, Ludwig trotting smartly at his heels.

"He should have saved his breath," said Mitch. "You don't have what it takes. Not a baby like you."

Hobie threw his leg over his bike.

"Running home to get your teddy bear?" Mitch threw the words like a punch.

"No. Just getting out of here so Duke doesn't catch your fleas!" Hobie stomped on the pedals and began to ride.

"Bluck, bluck, bluck!" Mitch called after him.

Hobie and Duke sped for home together, as they'd done hundreds of times before. But something was different for Hobie.

Like a record with a scratch in it, Mr. Rasmussen's story played over and over in his head.

And in his heart.

His are-you-doing-everything-you-can heart.

CHAPTER FOUR

A Dog for Defense

January 6, 1944

June stepped up on the bench to check the mailbox next to the front door. "A letter from Daddy!" She tippity-tapped in her red galoshes.

"Careful!" Hobie grabbed her arm so she wouldn't fall. Even though the letter was addressed to both of them, June tore it open.

"Oh, it's in cursive." She jumped down, holding the letter out to Hobie. "Read it to me!"

"Can we at least go inside where it's dry?" Hobie opened the door, grabbing Duke — with his favorite old tennis ball in his mouth — before he could run out.

"Come on, boy." Hobie tugged at Duke's collar. "We'll play later." Duke didn't care about the weather. In his doggy brain, rainy days were as good as sunny ones for a game of fetch.

Mom was volunteering at the hospital, so Hobie

had to make sure June hung up her wet coat and put her galoshes in the closet, and get her an after-school snack.

"Read the letter!" she repeated.

"Want some Ovaltine with it?" he asked. He was as eager as his sister to hear what Dad had to say, but sometimes things were better when you waited for them.

"Are there cookies?" June asked, clanking a saucepan out of the cupboard.

Hobie checked the pig cookie jar. Empty. "Graham crackers?" he suggested.

June sighed. "Oh, all right."

Hobie heated the milk and stirred in the Ovaltine powder. He ladled the warm drink into the mugs and set out a plate of graham crackers. "Ready?" he asked, picking up the letter.

"Wait! Wait!" June jumped up. "Kitty wants to hear, too."

She grabbed the doll from her bedroom and propped it up on the table. "Okay, we're ready."

Hobie unfolded the V-mail letter carefully so it wouldn't tear.

Dear Hobie and Junebug,

I was so proud to hear about those good report cards, my buttons nearly popped right off my uniform. Keep up the good work, but don't get too much smarter than your old dad, please.

Speaking of good work, I know you are both being troopers, pitching in at home and all. I'm going to have to ask you to be good soldiers awhile longer. Our favorite uncle has added a few more dances to my dance card. Don't you worry, the Lily Bess, Too is one tough bird. It can be 30 or 130. She'll do the job.

Someday, when you're older, I'd like to bring you here. They drink hot tea and eat cold toast, but they're good folks. They don't rattle easy, and that's something I admire.

This one's a groaner, but it's the best I've got for you this time: What do you do when your dog gets lost in the woods? Put your ear to a tree and listen for the bark.

Aim, fly, fight!
Love,
Dad

"What did Daddy mean?" June asked, nibbling the edge of a cracker. "About dancing?"

Hobie shoved his Ovaltine aside. "It means more missions." He wanted to crumple up the letter, throw it in the garbage. Dad was supposed to fly twenty-five missions. Twenty-five. And then he could come home. It wasn't fair!

June fussed with Kitty's hair. "How many more?" she asked.

"Who knows?" Hobie took another look at the letter. "Somewhere between thirty and a hundred and thirty." He couldn't breathe. Had to get out of there. He shoved his chair back. "Come on, Duke."

A volcano of mad erupted inside him, and the driving rain did nothing to cool it off. Hobie threw the ball, over and over again, as hard as he could. *Whump.* He hated those Nazis. *Whump.* He hated those Zeros. This darn war was all their fault. *Whump.* He even hated the Army, for making Dad fly more missions.

Duke dropped the ball at Hobie's feet. Water ran off his head as he bent over to pick it up. He hurled it again. *Whump.* He hated himself. For not doing everything he could. That was the strongest hate of all.

Mom pulled up to the curb and slid out of the car. "Hobie! You're soaked." She hustled him inside. "What were you thinking? This coat will never dry out in time for school tomorrow." She wrung it out over the sink, then hung it by the oil heater in the kitchen.

"Kitty's sad," June announced.

"About what?" Mom hung up her own coat and unpinned her hat.

"Daddy's letter."

Mom pivoted on her brown high heels. "You heard from Dad today?"

Hobie got the letter and handed it to Mom. She read it quickly, chewing all the lipstick off her lower lip.

"Well," she said, folding it back up. "We certainly need to send Dad a joke book. That was one of his worst." She put the letter in the basket with all the others. Then she tied on an apron and bustled around the kitchen, opening cupboards and banging pots and pans.

"Where are those green beans?" she asked, holding the can in her hand.

Hobie pointed that out to her. Mom pressed the can to her chest. Like she was praying.

June curled up on the sofa, with Kitty shielding her face so no one would see her thumb in her mouth. She hadn't sucked it since Dad first went off to the war. Seeing that was like getting jabbed with a fishhook, right in the heart. Even Duke could tell how sad June was; he curled up next to her the rest of the afternoon.

Hobie tried to eat the dinner Mom fixed, but mostly he just moved the mashed potatoes around on his plate. June jabbed green beans, one after another, into a mound of potatoes. "I made a porcupine," she said. "With green quills."

Instead of giving June a lecture about starving children in China and about not playing with her food, Mom just poured herself another cup of coffee. Her plate went untouched.

"Why can't this war be over?" June burst out, smashing the "porcupine" with her fork. Fat tears rolled down her cheeks.

"Come here, sweetie." Mom scooted her chair back from the table. June crawled up on Mom's lap, darkening the front of her blouse with tears.

Hobie cleared the table and fed Duke some of the scraps. He pretended to read his Hardy Boys book until it was time to take Duke out before bed. When they came back in, he could hear Mom and June in June's room.

"Sleep with me, Mommy?" June asked. The mattress springs creaked a little and then Mom was humming a lullaby.

Hobie flopped across his own bed, his heart as heavy as an anchor. On his dresser was a photo of Dad, Uncle Tryg, and Grandfather Hanson. It was taken before Uncle Tryg got his arm caught in the winch that one fishing season. The three of them were shaking hands with members of another crew, men they'd risked their own lives to rescue in a stormy sea.

Dad had a saying that courage doesn't always roar. But with the Hanson men, it seemed to roar. Hansons did what was needed. No matter how hard it was.

Hobie tossed and turned all that night, thinking and thinking. When he finally fell asleep, it seemed only five minutes had passed before he heard Mom making her breakfast coffee.

Hobie rolled over on his side, his arm dangling off the mattress edge, his fingers ruffling Duke's fur. Then he patted the bed. "Up." Duke stood and stretched, eventually obeying.

Hobie curled up next to his best friend and tried to think about what he was going to say to Mom and June.

When he told them of his decision, over their breakfast of oatmeal, June burst into tears. "No, no! Not Duke!" Then she ran to her room and slammed the door. It took Mom twenty minutes of talking to get her to come out and get ready for school.

There wasn't much time for Mom to say anything to Hobie. As he headed out the door, she grabbed him in a hug. "It's like I said," she told him. "You and your father. Peas in a pod."

Hobie didn't feel anything like Dad as he went through the motions of the school day. He jumped in his seat when Max tapped him on the arm. "We're supposed to exchange spelling tests," he said.

Hobie blinked. It was as if Max was speaking German. "What?"

Max held up a piece of paper. "You're supposed to correct my test and I'm supposed to do yours."

Hobie looked down. His test paper was completely blank. He handed it over, anyway.

Max's forehead wrinkled. "Are you okay?" he asked. "Maybe you need to go to the nurse?"

"I'm fine," Hobie lied, taking Max's test. Scooter would have made some sort of joke to cheer Hobie up, not asked if he wanted to go to the nurse. He might have even done his Mortimer Snerd imitation. That was one of Scooter's best.

When Hobie got his test back, he saw that Max had written the score at the top. But it was so small, you'd need a magnifying glass to see the zero.

He didn't feel so bad as he passed his paper forward when Mrs. Thornton called for them. Maybe there was more than one way to cheer a guy up.

As she had on the way to school, June refused to speak to Hobie on the way home. She shut herself up in her bedroom while Mom stood by as he dialed Mr. Rasmussen's phone number.

★ ★ ★

On Saturday, Hobie's stomach felt like it had the first time he went out on the *Lily Bess* and all he could do was hang over the side, as limp as seaweed. Every time he heard a car on the street, he jumped up and ran to the window. Duke began to whimper and pace.

"What time is it now?" Hobie rubbed Duke's belly.

"Ten minutes later than the last time you asked." Mom took another stitch in the sock she was darning for June. "Why don't you go play fetch?" she said. "It'd be good for the both of you."

When Duke saw the ball in Hobie's hand, he jumped straight up and flipped around.

Hobie threw. Duke fetched. He snagged the ball before it hit the ground every single time. Being fast would help keep him safe.

It started to drizzle as a Buick sedan idled to the curb. The quiet after the engine shut off tied another knot in Hobie's stomach.

Mr. Rasmussen slid out from behind the steering wheel. "There's our new recruit!"

Duke ran to greet him.

"Off," Hobie warned. Sometimes, with men, Duke would jump up. Duke obeyed, but wiggled close for a head pat. Mr. Rasmussen obliged.

"Hey, there, buddy," he said. "Good dog." He pulled a dog biscuit from his pocket. "May I give him this?"

Hobie nodded.

Duke happily crunched the treat while Mr. Rasmussen reached for a briefcase on the front seat.

Hobie patted his leg and Duke trotted over. They all went inside. Mr. Rasmussen settled on the sofa in the front room. Hobie sat on the footstool next to Mom's chair, his arm around Duke's neck. He felt like he was waiting his turn for a shot at the doctor's office.

June and Kitty sat as far across the room from Mr. Rasmussen as they could. Hobie could see June's thumb sneaking in and out of her mouth.

The first three times Mom offered, Mr. Rasmussen turned down coffee. But finally he said, "Well, if it's not too much trouble, I would enjoy a cup."

Mom carried in a tray with two cups and a plate of cookies. Hobie just wrapped his arm tighter around Duke's neck when Mom offered him one. June didn't take a cookie, either.

Mr. Rasmussen praised the cookies and coffee. Then he picked up his briefcase. "Shall we take care of the paperwork?" He unlocked the latches, reaching inside for a form that he held out to Hobie.

Hobie kept his arm around Duke's neck.

Mr. Rasmussen pulled a pen from his pocket. "You haven't changed your mind, have you?"

Yes, Hobie wanted to say. He had changed his mind a million times since they'd talked on the phone.

A thought occurred to Hobie. "What if the Army changes its mind?" he asked. "What if they don't want Duke?"

"Well, some dogs are rejected because of bad health. But Duke looks to be a perfect specimen." Mr. Rasmussen pursed his lips, thinking. "And, of course, some dogs aren't trainable, or have bad habits that can't be broken." He patted Hobie's arm. "Don't worry. Those instances are very rare."

Hobie hadn't been worried. He'd been hopeful. He sighed and took Mr. Rasmussen's pen. Using his best Palmer Method penmanship, Hobie filled out each line of the form. *Breed: German shepherd. Age: Three. Is dog afraid of noise? Storm shy? Gun shy?*

Hobie stopped, pointing to the last question. "Why do they ask this? Duke's going to be a guard dog here. Right?"

Mr. Rasmussen straightened his tie. "That's up to the Army, not Dogs for Defense. But most dogs *will* stay in the states."

Hobie held the pen over the paper. He was tempted to answer that "gun shy" question with a "Yes." Then Duke might be disqualified. But that would be dishonest. He wrote a shaky *No.*

The very last section asked, *Where should dog be returned after the war?* Hobie looked up at Mr. Rasmussen. "Doesn't everyone want their dog back?" he asked.

Mr. Rasmussen brushed cookie crumbs from his suit jacket. "Some people worry that the dogs won't know them. Or that it'd be too hard to undo the military training. So they let the handlers keep them."

Hobie sat back. Who would ever write down on this form that they didn't want their dog back? "Well, Duke is coming home. To me."

Mr. Rasmussen placed his hands on his thighs and leaned forward. "Son, I'm not going to make a promise I can't keep." He looked straight at Hobie. "The Army will do all it can to make sure Duke comes back to you. Absolutely all."

Hobie felt like he'd walked to the edge of a gang-plank. What was Mr. Rasmussen saying? That Duke might not come back? That he might not make it? His stomach felt seasick again.

"Do some of the dogs get . . . hurt?" Hobie asked.

"It has happened." Mr. Rasmussen kept Hobie's gaze. "It might help you to know that, since we've been using dogs, more and more soldiers are making it home to their families. Safe and sound."

That was good, of course, but it had never occurred to Hobie that Duke might be in danger.

Was it too late to change his mind? Hobie looked at June and then Mom and then over at the photo of Dad on the mantel. He was smartly dressed in his uniform, olive drab shirt and tie, with his hat tilted at a slight angle on his head. He looked all business, except for the familiar upward curve at each corner of his mouth. His eyes seemed to be looking directly at Hobie.

Hobie rolled the pen between his forefinger and thumb. More soldiers making it home safe and sound. That's what Mr. Rasmussen said. Soldiers and pilots. Safe and sound.

Hobie finished filling out the form and handed it back.

Mr. Rasmussen shook his hand. "I'll personally take Duke to the station." He smiled sadly. "He and Ludwig will ship out together, on a troop train. That'll be nice; they'll have some company. The Army will take good care of Duke, don't you worry." He said good-bye to Mom and June and then turned back to Hobie. "Are you ready?"

No, he wasn't ready. How could he be? But Hobie whistled and Duke followed him outside, to Mr. Rasmussen's car.

"Wait!" June called. "Kitty wants to say good-bye." She threw herself at Duke, her face buried in his ruff. Her shoulders bobbed up and down with silent sobbing.

"Okay, honey." Mom gently pulled her away. "Mr. Rasmussen needs to get going."

"In, boy." Hobie pointed to the backseat. Duke leaped right in. A car ride was a treat. He shifted from side to side, his nose making wet prints on the windows. Mr. Rasmussen would have to wash them later.

"Thank you for the coffee and cookies." Mr. Rasmussen slid onto the front seat and closed the door.

Duke put a paw up on the window. It looked like he was saying, "Hey, aren't you coming?"

Hobie lifted his hand, palm facing Duke. The command to sit. Duke sat. His brown eyes bored into Hobie's.

Hobie's stomach churned. What was he doing? Sending his dog away?

He looked over at Mom. She put her arm around his shoulder. It was for a good cause, right? For Dad.

"You'll be okay, boy," Hobie called out in a rusty voice. Duke would be okay. Would be safe.

That's what Hobie told himself as he stood on the sidewalk and watched Mr. Rasmussen drive away.

Drive away with his dog.

CHAPTER FIVE

Ghost Dog

January 12, 1944

Hobie rolled over, hung his arm off the bed, and reached for Duke.

It took him a moment to remember.

Duke was gone.

He got dressed, then reached under the bed for his sneakers. Duke's ball was in one of the shoes. Hobie picked it up and bounced it in his hand a few times before putting it in his dresser drawer. He finished tying his shoes. As he walked down the hall to the kitchen, he heard the echoes of Duke's nails clicking against the linoleum.

"Eat up." Mom set a bowl of Cream of Wheat in front of him. "You need your strength for that math test." She buttered a piece of toast for June.

The hot cereal had lumps that not even the raisins and brown sugar could disguise. Hobie swung his leg under the table and bumped only against air. Not against Duke.

And, even though he knew there would be nothing to see in the front room window, he still turned to look over his shoulder as he and June headed to school.

Hobie's brain was nowhere near his classroom. It was on a train, headed east, with a certain German shepherd. He wasn't even aware Mrs. Thornton was speaking until he heard Mitch's voice.

"He's probably up in the air with that Hop Harrigan." Mitch managed to make his laugh sound like a sneer.

"As I was saying, Hobie, you'd best get started on your math test." Mrs. Thornton leaned closer to him and lowered her voice. "Unless you're not feeling well."

"Need a pencil?" Max whispered, holding one out to him.

"Sure. Thanks." Math wasn't Hobie's strong suit under the best of circumstances. He hoped Mrs. Thornton didn't wear out her red pencil correcting his test.

When the recess bell rang, Hobie shuffled to the cloakroom, feeling a bit like one of Dr. Frankenstein's mistakes. Like he'd been sewn up with something missing inside.

"So, did you do it?" What had Mitch eaten for breakfast? Lutefisk? Hobie took a step back.

"Do what?" asked Catherine. She looked at Hobie.

"Give that dumb mutt away." Mitch blew a raspberry. "He's too much of a baby."

"Dumb mutt?" Max joined in.

"Duke?" Catherine pulled her coat close around her.

"What happened to Duke?" Some other kids gathered around.

Hobie fiddled with the buttons on his jacket. Stared at the floor. "He joined the Army," he said.

"You did do it!" Mitch exclaimed. "Never thought you had it in you."

"You gave Duke away?" Catherine scrunched up her face as if Hobie had said a curse word at school.

"I didn't give him away," Hobie said. "I loaned him. To the Army."

"Oh, Dogs for Defense," Preston Crane said. "I've heard of that."

"Yeah, the K-9 Corps," added Marty Reed.

"I would have done that, too, if I had a dog." Mitch was clearly not happy with the turn in the conversation.

"I wouldn't," Catherine said. "Give up my Molly? Not even for Uncle Sam."

Hobie couldn't read the look she gave him. He'd probably earned one more black mark in her book.

"That must've been hard," Max said. "Your dog."

Hobie glanced over at him. "Yeah. But it's for a good cause."

"That's right." Max lifted his jacket off the hook. "A good cause."

"Most of the dogs stay stateside," Hobie said, repeating what Mr. Rasmussen had told him.

"My brother's unit in Italy has messenger dogs," Mitch reminded Hobie. "And there are other kinds of dogs — mine sniffers, scout dogs —"

"But Hobie's dog will probably stay here," Max interrupted. "If most of the dogs stay here." He shoved his hands in his pockets.

"Right," said Hobie. At least someone was listening to him. Taking his side. "And when the war's over, I'll get him back."

Mitch cut a look at him. "You wish."

Those words fluttered in the air, like a moth with an injured wing. Kids stopped fastening coats, grabbing balls, and scuffling feet. The cloakroom was absolutely quiet. It bumped up against Hobie, making him feel even worse than he already did.

After a moment, someone dropped a ball, then shuffled his feet to grab it. Kids unfroze and ran outdoors.

Catherine tucked a big rubber ball under her arm.

"Sure you will," Catherine said with a confident bob of her head. "Now, come on. Max and I need you on our wall-ball team."

They convinced Preston to play, too. The four of them creamed Mitch's team.

As they scrambled inside after recess, smelling of the outdoors and wearing red cheeks and noses, Hobie actually felt good. As light as a balloon filled with helium. Not helium: hope.

The kind of hope that lets you believe that a war like the one the whole world was fighting would actually end and that both your dad and your dog would come home. And soon.

CHAPTER SIX

Dear Hobie

February 2, 1944

Hobie dropped June off at her Brownie meeting and then headed home, tugging up his jacket collar against the cold. A couple of blocks away, he passed a lady and a little girl. The little girl held one end of a leash. At the other end was a prancing Boston terrier.

"Heel, Suzy," the girl begged. The dog, Suzy, did everything but heel. She dragged the girl back and forth across the sidewalk until the lady grabbed the leash and snapped it like a whip.

"Bad Suzy," the lady said.

Hobie jumped as if he'd been snapped. Even when Duke was a puppy, Hobie never jerked him. Never hit him with a rolled-up newspaper. Hobie wouldn't like to be treated like that; why would Duke?

Duke. Hobie kicked at a rock on the sidewalk. He'd been Hobie's eighth birthday present, so rolypoly he looked like a stuffed toy. He'd jumped straight out of Dad's arms into Hobie's heart. Duke wore a white blaze on his chest and a little old man look on his mostly black face. Even as a pup, he'd been fearless, standing his ground with the neighbor's grumpy standard poodle. It was hard to remember life before slobbery tennis balls.

A sudden shower sent rivulets of water cascading down Hobie's neck. He picked up his pace, trying to outrun the rain and the fact that Duke was gone. Where was he? Was the Army treating him okay? Did he miss Hobie as much as Hobie missed him? A hundred questions ricocheted around in Hobie's aching chest.

He caught up with the rock and kicked it again. Hard.

It landed at the feet of another kid. A skinny kid with glasses and baggy corduroys. Max Klein.

"Sorry," Hobie called out. "That was an accident."

Max didn't seem to hear him. And Hobie quickly saw why.

Mitch.

Hobie stopped in his tracks.

"Who said you could walk here?" Mitch hollered at Max.

Max tugged at the canvas sack on his back and kept moving.

"I'm talking to you." Mitch shoved him. Hard. Max stumbled and fell back, crunching whatever was in the sack. He jumped up, and globs of slimy egg white and yellow yolks plopped off the seat of his pants.

Mitch barked out a laugh. "Hope you like your eggs sunny-side up."

"You're going to have to pay for these groceries," Max said.

"And who's gonna make me?" Mitch asked.

Hobie couldn't unstick his feet from the sidewalk.

Mitch curled his hands into fists. "You lousy Kraut." He shadowboxed at Max. Left. Right. Left.

"What's going on here?" A grandma lady marched right past Hobie, over to Max.

"Aw, my friend tripped." Mitch quickly picked up a can. "I was helping him." He held it out to Max, who snatched it away.

"You have a funny way of helping." The grandma picked up the egg carton, taking a quick look inside before closing the lid. "Looks like four Humpty Dumptys survived their fall," she said, handing the carton to Max. "It's a lucky thing eggs aren't rationed."

Max thanked her and she continued on her way.

"So long, traitor!" Mitch goose-stepped down the street in the opposite direction. Probably off to find a baby somewhere and steal its candy.

"Are you okay?" Hobie called as he walked closer.

Max tried to brush off his corduroys. "What am I going to tell Ma about these eggs?"

"The truth?" Hobie guessed.

Max gave him a look.

"Right." There was still a can of soup on the ground. Hobie picked it up. "Sorry," he said.

"For what?" Max took the can. "It wasn't your fault." He pulled the straps of the shopping bag over his shoulder. "See you at school."

The car was gone when Hobie got home; he found a note on the kitchen table. "Ran to Aunt Ellen's. I'll bring June home from Brownies." To fill up the quiet, he snapped on the radio, dialing in *Fibber McGee and Molly*. In this episode, Fibber was going to an aviation show. The announcer explained that Fibber was getting ready for it by reading a couple of flying magazines, then qualifying himself for a high rank in the HAF — the Hot Air Force.

Chuckling, Hobie opened the icebox to get himself some milk. His hand brushed against a carton of eggs. He pulled out the bottle and closed the door, standing there a moment. Had Max gotten into trouble at home over the eggs? Hobie didn't know why he worried about that, but he did. Even though he hadn't done anything.

Hobie stopped in mid-pour. That's right. He hadn't done anything. Anything mean.

Or anything good.

He set the bottle down with a *clunk*. He remembered that last week before Scooter moved. Hobie had accidentally bumped into Mitch in the lunch line. A tiny bit of gravy splashed on Mitch's shirt. It was an accident. But the guy wouldn't let it go. When Hobie went to sit down at the table, Mitch kicked the stool out from under him. Hobie crashed to the floor and his lunch tray went flying.

Mitch acted all innocent, so the lunch monitor didn't do anything but help Hobie clean up the mess. His rear ached from landing on it so hard. And he didn't have money to buy another lunch.

But Scooter shared his Spam sandwich and even did his canned-pea-booger trick to cheer Hobie up. That was Scooter. Always with the good ideas. Always the good friend. It was like the sampler Mom had hanging in the kitchen: *Friends double our joys and halve our sorrows.*

Hobie thought about that. His ideas were never as funny as Scooter's. But he did have an idea about Max. Hobie grabbed a couple of his comic books and stuffed them in a paper sack. He'd take them to school tomorrow, see if Max wanted to trade.

The back door banged open and Mom stepped inside. June was right on her heels, like Duke used to be on Hobie's.

"Somebody got some ma-ail!" Mom waved an envelope in the air.

It wasn't from Dad. Who, then? Hobie ripped it open.

Dear Hobie,

 I am writing you from Camp Lejeune, where I am now a member of the 3rd War Dog Platoon. Along with my friends Skipper, Missy, and Bunkie, I am working hard to whip these two-legged Marines into shape. My training buddy, Pfc. Marvin Corff, has managed to learn "sit" and "stay," but he's got a ways to go on the other commands. I'll have him trained up proper in no time.

They work us hard here, but I eat good and sleep in a nice kennel. I've got a brand-new leather collar and a serial number: 178. (Dogs don't get dog tags. Whaddya think of that?) And guess what? Today I learned how to maneuver an obstacle course with explosives going off all around. It was pretty exciting.

I hope you can write me back.

Your best pal,

Duke

P.S. Pfc. Corff here: Thank you for sending Duke. It's a dream to work with him. He's tops!

Hobie didn't understand. What was that about explosives? Why would a guard dog need to practice something like that? And Mr. Rasmussen never said anything about Duke joining the Marines. Or a War Dog Platoon. Never.

"Can you read it to us?" Mom asked.

Hobie did.

"I like the names of Duke's friends," said June. "Do you think we'll get to meet them someday?"

Mom tied on her apron. "Are you going to write back?"

Hobie stuffed the letter in his back pocket. "Maybe."

"That nice Marine took the trouble to let you know how Duke was doing." Mom rummaged around and found some paper and a pencil and handed them to Hobie. "And he's serving our country."

Hobie kicked his heels against the chair legs. "So's Duke," he said.

Mom raised an eyebrow. " 'Thank you for writing' would be a great way to start."

There was no arguing with Mom's eyebrow. Hobie put pencil to paper.

Dear Pfc. Corff,
  Thank you for writing.

Hobie kicked the chair legs again. What else was there to say except *I want my dog back*? He was supposed to be a guard dog. Safe at home. Mr. Rasmussen didn't tell him the truth.

June and Kitty were "helping" Mom start dinner. June was pretending she was the mommy and Kitty was the little girl.

"Oh, Kitty," June said in her mommy voice. "Duke will be back. Very soon. Just like Dad. It's all right." She cradled the doll in a hug.

June caught Hobie watching her. "Kitty's sad but I'm cheering her up," she explained. Then she walked over and leaned her head on Hobie's shoulder. She smelled of crayons and shoe polish.

She bent toward his ear. "Can I tell you a secret? I'm sad about Duke, too." A fat tear bounced down her cheek and landed on Hobie's letter.

June wiped at it. "I'm sorry. I'll get you another piece of paper."

He stopped her. "No. It's okay. Really." June had given him an idea. "I know you are going to get that spelling ribbon," he said.

Her eyes got as big as cookies. "I am?"

"Yep. Because you are so smart." He tapped her on the head gently with his pencil. "As smart as Duke."

She skipped off, dancing Kitty around the kitchen.

Hobie started writing again.

Do you have a sister, Pfc. Corff? Well, I do. She's a really good sister and she has been crying around the clock since Duke left. I wouldn't ask but my sister is so sad. Could you please send Duke back?

They take pets and other animals on the regular train. I know because my friend's grandmother comes to visit from Michigan every summer on the train and she always brings her dog, Winky. And he makes a lot more noise than Duke.

If it costs, I will pay you back.

Sincerely,

Hobie Hanson

"All done?" Mom asked.

Hobie sealed the letter up before she could ask to read it. He didn't want her to think he was a welcher or anything. But June was so sad! Hobie had to do whatever it took to get Duke back.

He licked a three-cent stamp, pasting it on with a cheerful pat. Duke was going to be home before they knew it.

"Done," he said.

CHAPTER SEVEN

Raising the Flag

March 25, 1944

June was having conniptions. "You're pulling too hard!" she complained.

Mom tugged another hank of June's wet hair around her finger and secured it with a bobby pin. "Don't you want to look your best tomorrow?"

June's lower lip poked out. "I think I'd look my best in a plain old ponytail." She waggled Kitty. "Kitty thinks so, too."

Hobie turned another page in the comic he'd traded with Max. Miss Milner, the school librarian, was a sport, letting Hobie and Max read in the library during rainy day recesses. Other kids had started bringing in their comics, too, and Miss Milner was talking about starting a club. Hobie didn't want a club. He just wanted to read comics.

"Ouch!" June hollered again. "Aren't you done yet?"

"Almost," said Mom. But she'd been saying that for half an hour.

Hobie was glad that all he'd needed to do was make sure his shoes were shined. Mom had even let him use Dad's brushes. This was the second year Dad would miss the Blessing of the Fleet. The Hansons never missed. There was even a photograph in the family album of a brand-new baby June there on the docks.

Every year since 1929, in late March, all the fishermen and their families would gather at Fishermen's Terminal. And every year, Pastor Haavik would choose one boat to represent the entire fleet, and he'd bless that boat.

This year, he'd picked the *Lily Bess*.

"How do those shoes look?" Mom asked, twisting another curl around her finger.

Hobie set down the comic and held them up for her to see.

"Dad couldn't have done a better job," she said. "I've ironed your white shirt, and laid out your tie."

"Tie!" He'd choke to death.

"Tie," said Mom firmly.

Hobie sighed. But not too loudly. At least he'd

only have to wear the tie for a few hours. June was going to have to sleep all night on those pokey bobby pins.

"Is that someone at the door?" Mom asked. "Go see."

Hobie scrambled up. A huge man filled the doorway.

"Just making sure you're going to be there tomorrow," said Uncle Tryg. He carried a box under his good arm. When he stepped inside, he held it out to Hobie.

"I got one of these for my boys," Uncle Tryg said, meaning Hobie's cousins Emil and Erik. "They don't have the patience. But I thought you might."

He handed Hobie a blue box stamped OFFICIAL AIR SCOUT SPOTTER MODELS. 25 CENTS. B-24. *THE LIBERATOR.*

"Dad's plane." Hobie ran his hands over the box.

June's lower lip stuck out even further. "What did you bring me?"

"Ah, my little pickled herring," Uncle Tryg said. "You don't think your favorite uncle would come empty-handed?" He reached into his pocket and pulled out a brand-new jump rope with colored handles.

"Oh, thank you!" June tried to reach for it, but Mom tugged her back down.

"We're not done here yet!" Mom said, fussing with a pin curl that had come loose.

"But I want to try out my new jump rope," said June.

"Not after I've gone to all this work on your hair," said Mom. "You can jump rope after the ceremony tomorrow."

"That's too long," June wailed.

Uncle Tryg patted his overcoat pocket. "I may have something that will sweeten the wait." He handed June a roll of Curtiss Fruit Drops. She tore it open and popped one in her mouth.

"What do you say?" Mom asked.

"Thank you!" June smacked on her candy. "Do you want one?" She offered the roll first to Mom and then to Uncle Tryg.

"I'll take one," said Hobie.

June made a face.

"June," said Mom.

"Oh, all right." June peeled the paper roll down farther, bypassing a cherry drop. "Here." She handed Hobie a green one. "I don't like this flavor."

"Gee, thanks." Hobie popped the candy in his mouth. Then he studied the cover of the model box. "This looks swell. Thanks, Uncle Tryg."

Mom came back from the kitchen with a cup of coffee and handed it to Uncle Tryg.

Hobie flipped the box around and read the back. A red, white, and blue message caught his eye:

BOYS! YOU CAN HELP WIN THE WAR!

Hobie leaned closer to read the fine print. THOUSANDS OF MODEL AIRCRAFT ARE NEEDED TO TRAIN NAVY, ARMY, AND CIVIL DEFENSE GROUPS. BLOCK HITLER — BUILD A PLANE!

"You could keep it," Uncle Tryg said, shrugging out of his overcoat. "Or donate it to the military. They're using them to train folks to look for certain plane silhouettes," he added.

Hobie hefted the box. "I don't get it." How could a model help the Army?

Uncle Tryg lifted his coffee cup high over Hobie's head. "If you hung that model on the ceiling, it would look like a B-24 flying about a mile up."

"Nifty!" Hobie decided right then. He would donate it when he finished. To do his part.

"You'll need some black paint," said Uncle Tryg. "But I thought your dad might have some in the basement."

"Would you like something to go with that coffee?" Mom asked. "I'm done here." She stretched a hairnet over June's head full of crisscrossed bobby pins. "You can go play now," Mom said. "But no jump roping!"

"The coffee hit the spot." Uncle Tryg set down his empty cup. "I best be on my way. See you tomorrow."

As soon as he left, Hobie ran to the basement. There was a small can of black paint at the back of Dad's workbench. He ran back upstairs. "I'll be in my room, Mom!" he called.

He carefully opened the model box with his pocketknife and read the instructions. Twice.

His bedroom door creaked open. "Whatcha doing?" June asked. She looked like some kind of space creature with those pins all over her head.

"Nothing." Hobie picked up a piece. Was that the right wing or the left?

"Can I help?" June bumped his elbow.

"No!" Hobie pushed her away.

"But I heard you and Uncle Tryg. This is Daddy's plane." She patted the box as if it were a pet. As if it were Duke.

Hobie sighed. "Okay. You can help. But you have to do exactly what I tell you." He set the pieces out on the desk. Some of them needed to be punched out of a thin wood frame. But they looked so flimsy. And breakable. Hobie picked them up and set them down again.

"I could punch them out," June offered. "I have lots of practice with my paper dolls."

Hobie hesitated. But her fingers were smaller than his. And she did have lots of paper dolls. He handed over the piece of wood and June gently pressed out the first piece.

"See?" she said. "Piece of cake. Want me to do the rest?"

Hobie's hand poised over the other pieces, then pushed them over. June finished that task while he started arranging the bigger pieces for assembling.

By the time they left for the Blessing of the Fleet on Sunday morning, bundled up against the cold March morning, both wings were sanded as smooth as Mom's fancy silk scarf. Hobie planned to glue them on that afternoon.

Mom, June, and Hobie made their way through the crowds, down the dock, passing boat after boat, breathing deep of salt and fish.

"Over here!" Aunt Ellen called, waving a handkerchief.

Mom took June's hand, and shivering in the raw air, they hurried to stand with Aunt Ellen.

"You'll come over after for coffee," Aunt Ellen said to Mom.

"Of course," Mom answered.

Hobie tried not to groan. He had hoped to work on the model that afternoon. "Coffee" at Aunt Ellen's would turn into a pinochle game for the grown-ups and then supper. It always did. Who knew when they'd get home?

"There's my boy!" Uncle Tryg came over and scooped Hobie in a bear hug. He turned to June. "And who is this movie star with you?" he asked.

June giggled, making her pin curls bounce. "It's me, Uncle Tryg. June."

"No!" Uncle Tryg looked very thoughtful. "Not Shirley Temple?"

June giggled again.

"May I borrow your brother, fair maiden?" Uncle Tryg asked. "I promise to bring him back."

"You may," June answered like a princess, curtsy and all.

"Come with me, young man." Uncle Tryg put his good arm around Hobie's shoulder. "The boys and I decided there was only one person to hoist the flag today." He tapped Hobie.

Hobie hesitated. "Are you sure?" He tugged at his necktie. "It's a pretty big deal. It seems like you should do it."

"Palmer would do the honors, if he were here, being the oldest." Emil and Erik were scuffling on the dock, and Uncle Tryg stepped over to separate them.

"He started it," Emil said.

"Uh-uh!" said Erik.

"Stow it," grumbled Uncle Tryg. "Oh, hello, Pastor!" He greeted Pastor Haavik, whose long nose was as red as the scarf wrapped around his neck.

"God bless, Tryg!" Pastor Haavik shook hands with all of the Hanson crew. Then he pulled a small purple flag from his pocket.

"I remember your father when he was your age,"

71

the pastor said to Hobie, handing him the flag. "He and Tryg were like those two —" He tilted his head toward Erik and Emil. "It's a wonder your grandfather had any hair at all, with the trouble they gave him."

Hobie glanced over at his cousins. Emil sneaked a punch to Erik's arm. Erik's shoe landed on top of Emil's foot. He had a hard time picturing Dad and Uncle Tryg acting like that.

"Let us pray."

Uncle Tryg and the other men removed their hats. Pastor Haavik bowed his head, and the crowd quieted. For a small man, he had a big voice. And the water helped carry it over the docks. "We ask that you keep this boat, the *Lily Bess*, and each crewman upon it safe during this fishing season. Likewise, we petition for the safety of every boat and every man in the Seattle fleet. The sea is big, oh Lord, but you are bigger. Amen."

Hobie stood there uncertainly a moment after the prayer finished. He didn't want to do the wrong thing.

"Up you go, boy!" Pastor Haavik waved his hand, and Hobie scrambled across the gangplank to the boat's deck. He clipped the flag on the lines and hoisted it up, up, up. When it bumped at the top of the pole, the crowd cheered. His hands ached from the cold, but Hobie felt warm inside. If only Dad's was one of the faces there on the dock.

He made his way back across the gangplank and leapfrogged to the dock.

"Good job, Hobie." Uncle Tryg shook his hand and then pointed to the flag. "When the season's over, we'll send that to your dad," he said.

"He might be home before then," Hobie said.

"Right you are." Uncle Tryg tugged on the brim of his hat. "There's always hope with a line in the water," he said.

Before Hobie could figure out what that meant, Emil grabbed his arm. "Race you to the end of the dock!" Hobie tore off after his cousins, the three of them dodging this way and that through the departing crowd.

At Uncle Tryg's, the cousins played a rousing game of Chinese checkers — June won — while the adults drank coffee and talked. Aunt Ellen's butterscotch pie almost made up for not being able to work on the model.

They came home to find an envelope wedged behind the screen door. *Delivered to my house by mistake* was penciled on the front. Hobie's heart jumped when he saw it was addressed to him. From Camp Lejeune. He ran to his room to read it.

Dear Hobie,

   I am wagging my tail because Marv and I passed our training with flying colors. I never doubted that I'd pass, but Marv was another question altogether. The hardest thing (for me, not Marv) was learning not to bark. Especially during field exercises.

   Your pal,

   Duke

   P.S. Corff here: I don't have a little sister, but if I did, I hope I could be the kind of big brother you are. I hate to break a kid's heart, but Duke and I are a team now. I promise I will bring Duke back to you — and your sister — as soon as I can.

Hobie crumpled the letter and tossed it in the waste bin.

His plan hadn't worked. Now what was he going to do to get Duke back?

CHAPTER EIGHT

Plan B

April 3, 1944

Mom sent Hobie on an errand right after school. "I'm out of eggs and I need some for this new recipe I got from Aunt Ellen. Codfish casserole; doesn't that sound tasty?"

It didn't sound tasty to Hobie, but Aunt Ellen was a good cook so it was probably okay. Of course, Mom thought of a few other things she needed at Lee's. Hobie slipped the straps of a canvas shopping bag over his shoulder and jumped on his bike.

He scarcely felt the rain spitting down on him as he pedaled. His mind kept bumping against the topic that had been like a pebble in his shoe over the last few weeks: what to try next to get Duke home. Last night, he'd been so preoccupied while he was working on the spotter model, he'd nearly glued the wings on upside down. June had stopped him before he ruined everything.

Hobie parked his bike outside Lee's Grocery, a little store that was really Mrs. Lee's house. Duke used to rest his nose on the front porch railing when he'd come with Hobie. Mrs. Lee had a strict rule against dogs in the store.

"Well, if it isn't my favorite customer." Mrs. Lee wiped her hands on her apron. "What have you got for me today?"

"Fresh out of jokes," he apologized. He wasn't in the joking mood.

"Well, doggone it," she said. Then she slapped the counter. "Doggone it. Get it?"

Hobie forced a smile.

Mrs. Lee straightened a display of cans. "Taste-well soup's on sale, three for a quarter."

"Here's Mom's list," he said, handing it over.

Mrs. Lee read, then began assembling. A three-pound tin of Spry shortening, a package of tea, a packet of sandwich cookies, and, from the icebox, a dozen eggs. Hobie put the groceries in the canvas sack and then counted out the ration stamps.

Mrs. Lee tallied up the bill. "That'll be a dollar sixty-eight," she said.

Hobie handed over the stamps and the money.

She handed back two cents in change. "Tell your mother I pray for your father each night."

"I will." Hobie put the pennies in his pocket.

Mrs. Lee fished two root beer barrels from one of the glass jars on the counter. "One for June, too," she said, handing him the candies.

Hobie added them to the pennies in his pocket. "Thank you!" As he headed out the door, Max was heading in, holding the arm of an old man with white fuzzy duckling hair. Hobie held the door for them. He and Max hung out together nearly every day at lunch, but it felt funny seeing him out of school. Kind of like running into a teacher at the movie theater or something.

"I've got those pigs' feet, Mr. Klein!" Mrs. Lee called out when she saw them. She reached under the counter and brought out a large glass jar.

The old man moved very slowly, and his hands trembled a bit as he reached out for it. "Oh, you are a dumpling, Mrs. Lee."

Mrs. Lee chuckled. "What else can I get you today?"

While the old man and Mrs. Lee talked, Hobie turned to Max. "Pigs' feet?" he asked.

"Even worse," Max said. "They're pickled."

They both made faces and then cracked up.

"Grandpa says I'll like them when I get older," Max said.

"Kind of makes you not want to grow up," said Hobie. "That's your grandpa?"

"He lives with us." Max stepped farther inside the store. "I better help him."

"See you tomorrow," Hobie said, slipping through the door.

"My uncle sent me a new comic we can read," Max called after him.

Hobie started for home. The rain had let up, but there were plenty of puddles to splash through as he rode. Pigs' feet! Poor Max.

A block from Lee's, he saw the little girl with the Boston terrier again. There had been no improvement in the obedience department. The dog was zigzagging her across the sidewalk, and through every single puddle. When a squirrel leaped down from a tree, the dog bolted after it, turning the little girl into a human kite.

Hobie didn't know who he felt more sorry for — the girl or the dog.

Without warning, the dog changed course and dashed right in front of Hobie. He slammed on his brakes, jerking to a stop.

"Watch what you're doing!" he shouted at the girl.

She tugged on the leash. "I'm trying," she said. "But Suzy won't mind." The girl wiped her nose on her coat sleeve. "Mother says if I don't get her trained soon, she's going back to the pound."

Suzy snuffled at Hobie's leg.

"What have you done to train her?" Hobie asked.

"I make her wear a leash," the girl said. "And I tell her no."

"Let me try something." Hobie set his bike down and fished a cookie from the packet in the shopping bag.

"Here, Suzy." He broke off a tiny piece and let Suzy sniff it. Then he gave it to her.

"She likes it!" the girl exclaimed.

"Cookies aren't great for dogs," Hobie admitted. "But that's all we've got." He took the leash from the girl and positioned Suzy next to his left leg. She stared at him as if he were some kind of doggy treat dispenser.

"Suzy, sit." Hobie waited. Suzy didn't sit.

"Sit, Suzy!" the girl said.

"Just one of us at a time." Hobie tried it again. "Sit."

Suzy licked her chops, hoping for a cookie.

"Nope," Hobie said lightly. He pressed gently on her back end. "Sit."

Suzy sat. She got a treat. She looked up at Hobie, licking her chops again.

"She did it!" the girl exclaimed.

"Now, she needs to do it about fifty times," Hobie said. "And that's no joke."

When it seemed like Suzy had gotten the idea, Hobie turned leash and cookie over to the girl.

"She's sitting!" the girl said. "She's minding!"

"Have her do it again," Hobie said, "but this time no cookie. Just pet and praise her."

The girl did what Hobie said. "She's still minding!" She did a little hop. "Wait till I show Mother!"

Hobie gave her a quick lesson on stay and heel. "Work with her every day." He rubbed Suzy's head. "You're a good dog, aren't you, girl?"

Suzy flopped down on her back for a belly rub. Hobie gave her one. "I better get going," he said.

"Come, Suzy." The little girl started for home,

Suzy prancing smartly at her side. After a few paces, Suzy zigged in front of the girl again. "Oops!" the girl giggled.

"Practice makes perfect!" Hobie called after her. That's something she would've figured out if she'd gone to the library and checked out even one book on dog training. Hobie slung the grocery sack over his shoulder and picked up his bike. Suzy wouldn't have to go to the pound. But it was going to take more time to break her of her bad habits.

Hobie had to admit that, despite all the time he'd worked with Duke, he never could cure him of his weakness for squirrels. It was Duke's only bad habit.

Bad habit! Hobie slammed on his brakes. He remembered something Mr. Rasmussen had said that day. That some dogs were returned because of bad habits that couldn't be broken.

Hobie cranked on the pedals. Not to beat out the rain this time, but to get home as fast as he could.

He had another letter to write.

"Where's the fire?" Mom asked when he burst in the house. "Oh, my goodness. You're drenched." She took the groceries from him. "Go change and I'll make you some hot Ovaltine to warm you up."

After putting on dry clothes, Hobie grabbed some stationery. With the mug of Ovaltine at his elbow, he began to write.

Dear Pfc. Corff,

There's one thing I forgot to tell you about Duke. If he sees a squirrel, he can't think about anything else. He will run after it no matter what. I have tried for three years to break him of that bad habit.

I wouldn't want him to cause you a problem. So, you should probably send him back.

Very truly yours,

Hobie Hanson

He sealed the envelope, pasted on a stamp, and ran to the postbox on the corner.

Why hadn't he thought of this sooner?

No matter. Hobie dropped the letter in the mail slot.

Duke was as good as his again.

CHAPTER NINE

A Spot of Trouble

April 24, 1944

Mom and June were thrilled with their latest letters from Dad. But Hobie's made him squirm.

Dear Hobie,

When I said you would need to be the man of the house while I was gone, I had no idea how much of a man you would be. Duke means so much to you. Loaning him to the war effort is one of the bravest things I've heard of.

I know it's easy to think of bravery as something big and bold. But the kind of bravery you showed requires putting others before yourself. Not many people can be that kind of brave.

This has to be short — duty calls. But I couldn't rest tonight until I let you know how proud I am of you.

Tell Mom that Duke deserves his own service
flag hanging in the window!

I love you, son.

Dad

Hobie put Dad's letter in his dresser drawer. At the back, behind his socks.

"Are you feeling okay?" Mom asked at dinner. "I thought chipped beef on toast was your favorite."

Hobie spooned up a bite and put it in his mouth. The gravy tasted like glue but it had nothing to do with Mom's cooking. He forced himself to swallow.

"I'm fine," he said.

But he wasn't. Dad wouldn't be so proud if he knew about the letters to Pfc. Corff. That wasn't putting others first. That was being selfish. Wanting Duke back.

"May I be excused?" he asked.

Mom frowned at his still-full plate. "No dessert," she said.

"I know." Hobie cleared his dishes, scraping the uneaten dinner into the garbage.

"I ate all my dinner," June said. "So I get dessert. Right, Mommy?"

Hobie didn't wait to hear Mom's answer. He made his way down the hall to his room, where he grabbed a Green Lantern comic book from the desk. Dad wouldn't have to know about the letters, he told himself as he lay on his bed, flipping the pages. Besides, didn't Dad always say he would love Hobie no matter what he did?

Hobie flopped over on his stomach. Dad would still love him all right. But be proud of him?

He turned another page in the comic. Alan Scott, the Green Lantern, had just discovered he could be weakened by wood. And the bad guy was going after him with a wooden club. It didn't look good for the Green Lantern, not even with his magic ring.

If he had known about that weakness ahead of time, he could have prepared for it somehow. Maybe some kind of shield. What else that might work against wood? Fire? So if the Green Lantern had a shield, or a torch, the bad guy wouldn't be winning.

That was why it was a good thing that he'd told Pfc. Corff about Duke. To make sure the bad guys wouldn't have the advantage. The Marines *needed* to know about Duke's bad habit. It might mean life or death to some soldier. Hobie closed the comic book and got ready for bed.

Though he tried to concentrate on other things, like what to plant in the Victory garden come summer, or Suzy and the little girl, or even pickled pigs' feet, Dad's words were the last things he thought of before falling asleep.

"Can I carry the model?" June poked her head in Hobie's bedroom bright and early the next morning. "I helped."

"But it's *mine*." Hobie carefully put the B-24 in an old shoe box. When Mrs. Thornton had learned he'd been working on it, she'd asked him to bring it to school when it was finished. Now, the black paint was completely dry. It was safe to take it in.

"You can carry something of mine," June persisted.

"June, let your brother alone," Mom called. "Come here and I'll braid your hair."

Hobie munched a bowl of Wheato-Naks while Mom worked on June's hair.

"Mommy, did you know this week's spelling words are just like us?" June asked.

"Really?" Mom wound a rubber band at the bottom of the first braid.

June nodded. "Oops. Sorry."

"Hold still now." Mom rewound the rubber band.

"This week's list has 'mother,' 'brother,' and 'sister.' No 'father.'" June made a face as Mom tugged the second braid into shape.

"We have a father," Hobie said.

"Well, he's not here," said June. "Just like 'father' is not on my spelling list." She stuck her tongue out at Hobie.

"There you go." Mom patted the braid. "All finished." She gave June a kiss on the forehead. "Your dad is with you, no matter what." She tapped June lightly on the chest. "Right here, in your heart."

"I don't like it that both Dad and Duke are gone." June leaned into Mom for a hug. "Do you?"

"Life is full of things we don't like," Mom said. "But what matters is our attitude." She gave June another hug. "Would some icebox cookies help with your attitude?"

June's head bobbed up and down.

"I'll have some for you this very afternoon." Mom gave June a pat on the rump. "Now you two better get going or you'll be late."

When Hobie dropped June off at her classroom, she grabbed his arm. "Dad's right here," she said, patting her chest. "Right?"

June looked so small and worried that Hobie was tempted to give her a hug. But not at school. He tugged one of her braids. "Tell you what, I'll let you take a turn carrying the model home after school. How's that sound?"

"Great!" June skipped off into her classroom, and Hobie could hear her saying, "Miriam, Miriam. Guess what I get to do!"

When she saw the model, Mrs. Thornton acted like Hobie had invented the lightbulb or something.

"Oh, this is wonderful," she said, admiring it from all angles. "I'm sure our arithmetic can wait a few minutes." She pushed some papers aside on her desk. "I know *I'd* love to hear Hobie tell us more about his project." She sat down, her face aglow with encouragement.

Hobie scratched his arm. "There's not much to

tell." He scratched the back of his neck. All this attention was giving him a rash. "My uncle brought me this model because it's the kind of plane my dad flies. A B-24."

"The Liberator!" Marty called out. He was a fiend for planes.

Hobie nodded. "Yeah. I mean, yes." Mrs. Thornton insisted on good grammar. "The Army and the Navy and the Civil Defense use these models to train spotters. So they can pick out a plane from a mile off."

"That's so interesting." Mrs. Thornton clasped her hands together.

"And I'm going to donate this to the Army," he said. "Because of my dad."

"I'm sure he'll be very pleased to know that. What you've done is quite remarkable." Mrs. Thornton patted Hobie on the shoulder. "And now I'm certain you young citizens are eager to get to that quiz on long division!" She stood up.

"Hobie, why don't you put your model on the back counter for safekeeping?"

Hobie did and they moved on to the quiz. That was not as remarkable as the model.

Mrs. Thornton seemed genuinely sad about Hobie's 79 percent.

Let's work together on a multiplication refresher, she'd written across the top.

Hobie didn't know why he had to learn long division. Dad never used it on the *Lily Bess*. Neither did Uncle Tryg. Or Mom. But it was important to Mrs. Thornton. She stayed in with him at recess to review his times tables.

Hobie did okay until he got to the sevens.

"I have trouble with those, too," Mrs. Thornton confessed.

"You do?"

She put her finger to her lips. "This will be our secret, okay?"

"Okay." Hobie felt a little better.

"Sometimes, it's even hard to do the twos and threes," she said. "Thinking about Neil." She looked over at the photo on her desk. Her husband, in uniform.

Hobie erased one of his wrong answers. "I miss my dad, too. I want him to come home." He hoped he didn't sound like too much of a baby.

"Me, too." She patted the locket at her throat. "I

mean, your dad and my husband." Then she turned her red pencil over and over again. "I want them all to come home."

Hobie wasn't sure, but he thought he saw tears sparkling in her eyes. "They say the war will be over soon."

Mrs. Thornton's smile wobbled. "I hope so. I certainly hope so."

Hobie could hear his classmates in the cloakroom. Recess was over. "I'll put these away." He picked up the flash cards.

Hobie set them on the math shelf in the supply closet. As he closed the door, he saw Mitch bump against the spotter model.

It crashed to the floor. The right wing sheared clean off.

Hobie ran over. "You did that on purpose!"

"No, I didn't." Mitch held out his hands. "Honest."

Mrs. Thornton bustled to the back of the room. "What's going on?"

Max picked up the plane. Before Hobie could say anything, Mitch jumped in. "I accidentally bumped this off the counter."

Hobie glared at him.

"Oh, how awful." Mrs. Thornton looked at Hobie. "Can it be repaired?"

"It's ruined." Hobie felt sick. He needed to go to the nurse.

"My grandfather might be able to fix it," Max offered. "He's a woodworker."

Mrs. Thornton nodded. "Well, that's a wonderful suggestion."

Hobie looked at Max. The pigs' feet grandfather. Who looked a little like Santa Claus. "How could he fix this?" He waved his hands over the mess.

"You never know," Max said. "Come over and see."

Mrs. Thornton started back for her desk. "Oh, Mitch, even though it was an accident, you still owe Hobie an apology."

"I'm sorry about your plane," Mitch said.

Hobie accepted the apology. For Mrs. Thornton. How could he believe anything that came out of Mitch Mitchell's mouth? Hobie sat at his desk sending air arrows at Mitch the rest of the day.

"Walk home with me," Max said after the last bell rang. "Grandfather can take a look."

"I have to take June home first," said Hobie. "I'll come over after that."

But not even the temptation of icebox cookies could keep June home when she learned what had happened.

"I don't see the harm of her going along," said Mom.

Hobie couldn't believe it. It was like June was an anchor he had to carry everywhere.

"Mom!" he said. "She wasn't invited. Just me." Scooter had three little sisters, and he never had to drag any of them anywhere.

"I helped build the model," June said. "I should get to go, too."

"She does have a point, Hobie." Mom hesitated. "Just this once. After this, Hobie goes to Max's house on his own."

Hobie groaned. As if there would be another time after this. Why did he have to have a little sister anyway?

"Use your company manners," Mom said. She wrapped some icebox cookies in wax paper. "And take these." She handed the package to June.

Hobie walked as fast as he could to the Kleins'. Still, June's little legs managed to keep up. She turned shy when they got to the house, though, ducking behind Hobie when Max answered the door. Some kind of orchestra music was playing on a record player in the background.

"This is my kid sister, June," Hobie said. "And these are from my mom."

"Come on." Max took the package of cookies. "My grandfather's workshop is around here." He led the way to a small building in the backyard. Hobie felt a little shy, too, now that he was here at Max's house. It wasn't noisy, like Scooter's, with all his sisters giggling and gabbing.

"Opa?" Max called. "My friends are here."

"*Ja?*" Max's grandfather shuffled to the door of the shop. "*Kommt doch rein.*"

Hobie stepped inside, June right on his heels. The shop smelled of pitch and shavings and licorice. Familiar smells.

A wooden worktable ran the length of the far ~ns of glass jars filled with nails and .eir lids from the bottoms of three .bove the worktable. The short walls of the shop were covered with Peg-Board, from which hung an astonishing assortment of neatly arranged tools. Dad would have pronounced it shipshape.

"This is Hobie, and this is June," Max introduced them. "And this is from their mom." He unwrapped the cookies and offered them around.

"*Danke.*" Max's grandfather ate his cookie in two bites. "Now, what is your trouble?" he asked.

Hobie felt better that the grandfather was speaking English. But it was confusing. Getting help from someone who was from Germany when Dad was over there fighting the Germans. Life could sure be complicated sometimes.

Hobie pulled the two pieces of the model from the box. "This," he said.

Grandfather Klein brushed his hands off before taking the model from Hobie.

"Uh-huh." His spectacles slid down his nose. "This. No problem." He slipped on a pair of safety goggles and drilled one hole in the body of the plane and a matching hole in the edge of the wing.

"Max, bring me some of that doweling there." He pointed at a coffee can that looked like it was filled with different-sized arrows, without the points.

"Will this do?" Max handed him a very thin piece.

"*Gut.*" Grandfather Klein picked up a small saw and cut the dowel to size. After squeezing a bead of smelly glue on either end, he pushed the bit of dowel into the hole he'd drilled in the body. Then he pushed the wing-hole onto the protruding tip of the dowel.

"Like new!" He handed the plane back to Hobie.

"That's amazing." It did look good as new. "Thank you. Thanks a lot."

Max's grandfather stepped over to a Crescent coffee can, removed the lid, and held it out to Hobie and June. Hobie glanced over at Max.

Max grinned. "Don't worry. It's not you-know-what." He made a soft oinking sound.

"Licorice!" exclaimed June. "Yum." She and Hobie each took a piece. Hobie sniffed his. Salty. And as hard as a piece of dried bubble gum. Not soft like the licorice he sometimes bought at Mrs. Lee's.

"You must come again," said Grandfather Klein. "Max would like that. *Ja?*"

"I would like that, *ja*," said June.

Hobie tapped her. "He was talking to me," he said.

June had put a piece of licorice in her mouth, so she couldn't answer back. Mr. Klein laughed at the expression on her face.

As soon as they were outside, June spit out the licorice. "I don't like that kind," she said. "But I like Mr. Klein. He looks like Santa. *Opa.*" She tried out the word. "Opa Klein. And I like your friend Max, too."

Hobie stopped for a second. His friend Max? Max, a friend? He tried that thought on for size. And liked it. Maybe Max wasn't a drum major, like Scooter, directing Hobie's life this way and that. But maybe there were different kinds of friends. Quieter kinds. "They're both okay, in my book," Hobie said. He whistled all the way home, carrying the model with care.

"Mail call," Mom sang out when the front door creaked open. "For Mr. Hobie Hanson."

Hobie took the letter from her. It was from Pfc. Corff. He paused before opening it, mentally crossing his fingers. Had his plan worked?

There was only one way to find out. Hobie took a deep breath and opened the envelope.

Dear Hobie,

We got our orders. I can't tell you what they are exactly, but I can tell you that my tail's wagging because we're headed to California. I hope I get to meet Lassie!

Your pal,
Duke

The letter ended with a P.S.:

You don't have to worry about a thing with Duke. He is the most disciplined dog in the unit. Even if we run into any squirrels where we're going, I don't think he'll pay them any mind. But it was good of you to be concerned.

Semper Fi,
Pfc. Marvin Corff

Hobie folded the letter back up. All the lightness of the afternoon had turned to lead.

The only good news in the letter had been about California. That was about as far away from the war as you could get.

At least Duke would be safe.

CHAPTER TEN

A Day to Remember

May 29, 1944

After a few weeks without any mail from Dad, a bunch of letters arrived all at once. One for Hobie, one for June, and three for Mom.

"Read it to me!" June begged Hobie, waving her letter around. "Wait. Kitty wants to hear, too." She ran and got her doll. "Now we're ready."

Dear Junebug,

I am proud of you, working so hard for the spelling ribbon. Though I'm pulling for you to win, what matters most is how much you have learned.

The cookies you and Mom sent arrived and were gone within minutes. I could've eaten the whole batch myself, but I refrained and shared them with my crew. They request oatmeal cookies the next time.

Since you are such a good speller, this question will be easy for you to answer: How many letters are there in the alphabet?

Brush your teeth, say your prayers, and mind your mother.

Love,

Daddy

"What a silly question Daddy asked," June said. "Everyone knows there are twenty-six letters in the alphabet."

Dad had played this trick on Hobie in his younger days.

"But that's not the answer," he said.

June recited the alphabet, counting out each letter on a finger. She went around her left hand five times, with one finger left over. "Twenty-six!" she insisted.

Hobie took a pencil and a piece of paper. He wrote the words "the alphabet" on the paper and pushed it toward June.

She scrunched up her face, looking at it this way and that.

"Oh!" she exclaimed. "Now I get it! Eleven!" She grabbed another piece of paper. "I have to write Daddy back right away."

Hobie had to hand it to June. She figured out that riddle faster than he had.

He picked up his own letter from Dad and began to read.

Dear Hobie,

Just when I think you can't make me more proud, you tell me about making a spotter model. My bombardier said he thought it was mostly high school kids assembling them. He was quite impressed. I may be wearing the uniform, but you are certainly one of Uncle Sam's soldiers.

I like many things about the people here, but their menus I will gladly leave behind. I would take lutefisk over kidney pie any day. And you know how fond I am of lutefisk!

When Uncle Tryg gets back from Alaska this summer, why don't you ask him if there are any chores you can do? It would give your mother heart palpitations were you to go out on the Lily Bess, but there are plenty of jobs that can be done from the safety of dry land. It would mean a lot to me if you could lend a hand, since I can't be there.

All right, my boy. Here's a new one for you. It's a knee-slapper, in my book: What happens

when it rains cats and dogs? (You might step in a
poodle.)

    Aim, fly, fight!
    Love,
    Dad

Dad's joke was pretty lame, but Mrs. Lee would get a kick out of it next time Hobie went to the store. Hobie skimmed the letter again. Aunt Ellen made lutefisk every Christmas, but Dad wouldn't touch it. "It tarnishes the silver," he'd say. "Think what it does to the innards!" Aunt Ellen would argue that every good Swede eats lutefisk, and Dad would say, "Well, it's a good thing I'm Norwegian, isn't it?" Hobie suspected Aunt Ellen only served the smelly stuff to get Dad's goat.

The part of the letter that really jumped out, though, was where Dad wrote about Hobie helping with the *Lily Bess.* Neither Erik nor Emil had been allowed to work on her until they were thirteen. Hobie was not yet twelve. He took a deep breath. It was like he'd won a ribbon, himself, for Dad to say what he had.

Hobie's top dresser drawer held quite a collection

of letters. He tucked this one from Dad in, along with the others, including a nice stack from Duke, too. Well, from Pfc. Corff. He hadn't heard from them in a while. He picked up the letter they'd sent back in February.

Dear Hobie,

I don't want you to think it's all work, work, work for me here. We dogs had a bit of fun the other day with some paratroopers. Seemed they thought the war dog unit was a bunch of hooey and had been digging at us but good — howling whenever they saw our handlers, throwing hot dogs at them, and generally being jerks.

Then they got the bright idea to sneak into our unit one night, thinking to cut the ropes on some of our guys' tents. Those jumpers didn't count on me and Big Boy. We kept them at bay until Marv and the rest rounded them up and sent them on their way. I don't think they'll be any trouble anymore.

I've been doing all that's been asked of me. Some days, Marv can barely stand on his two legs at the end of a training session. But I have the zip to chase a ball for hours, no matter what.

Your pal,

Duke

P.S. Hobie — wish you could have seen the look on those paratroopers' faces when Duke and Big Boy took them down. Two dogs. Six men. No problem!

Semper Fi — Marv

Hobie could very well imagine the looks on those troopers' faces. He'd seen a similar look on Mitch's that time in the park. He wouldn't want to be on the receiving end of Duke's bad mood. But it sure sounded like those guys deserved it!

He riffled the edges of the envelopes lined up in his drawer. He was supposed to take something to school tomorrow, for the class Memorial Day program. The letters from Dad seemed too personal. There were the letters from Pfc. Corff, but what if someone — like Mitch — thought Hobie really believed Duke was writing to him? He'd never live it down.

But it wasn't a bad idea. Sharing about Duke. Hobie bet no one else would think about remembering the four-legged members of the military. Mrs. Thornton might even give Hobie extra credit.

He pulled out the Dogs for Defense pamphlet Mr. Rasmussen had given him, and grabbed Volume Five of the World Book encyclopedia from his bookshelf. It had great pictures of all kinds of dogs. Hobie slid onto his desk chair and began pulling together some notes. Across the top of a piece of paper he wrote, *K-9s for Uncle Sam*. K-9s. Canines.

Mrs. Thornton would like that. She'd like it a lot.

"Welcome to the Room 31 Memorial Day celebration," Mrs. Thornton announced the next morning. No one was surprised that her contribution was another photograph of her husband. He looked like a movie star, too, but not a heartthrob like Cary Grant. More like Jimmy Stewart.

Several students also brought pictures of fathers and uncles.

"This is my big brother, Mike." Mitch waved a photo around without even waiting to be called on. "He just made Sergeant First Class." There wasn't much resemblance between the two brothers. For one thing, Mike wore a big smile. Looked almost friendly. "He's whipping the Nazis in Italy," Mitch boasted before sitting down.

Catherine Small showed off a muffler she was knitting for one of "the boys." "This is the fifth one I've made," she said. "I knit every day, after school, while I listen to the radio. My favorite shows are *Dick Tracy* and *Jack Armstrong*."

"What a lovely gesture, dear," said Mrs. Thornton.

Hobie never knew girls liked those kinds of shows, too. Come to think of it, Catherine wasn't really the type to listen to anything like those soap operas Scooter's sisters went crazy over.

Preston Crane, the class whiz kid, brought in a scrapbook he'd made of war headlines and articles, divided into color-coded sections.

"My goodness, this is thorough," said Mrs. Thornton. Preston puffed up like he'd won the World Series, single-handed.

Mitch raised his hand. "We haven't heard from Max," he said in a weaselly voice.

"He was waiting his turn," Hobie called out. Why did Mitch have to be so mean to Max? "And it's way better than a picture," he added. Max had given him a glimpse in the cloakroom before school.

Maybe what he'd brought would shut Mitch up for once.

"Max, would you like to share now?" Mrs. Thornton asked.

He pushed his chair away from his desk and pulled something from a paper sack. "My cousin sent me this belt buckle made from a coconut shell." Max held it up. "He's on the USS *Enterprise*," he added. "A radio operator. He was there." He paused. "In Pearl Harbor. He saved two of his buddies after the attack."

"Oh, dear," said Mrs. Thornton. She dabbed her nose with a lacy handkerchief. "You must be so proud of him."

"Yes." Max stared straight at Mitch. "Yes, we are."

Right then, Dorine Bunch, one of the quietest kids in the class blurted out: "I miss Tomiko."

It might have been the longest speech Hobie had ever heard her give. And he'd known her since kindergarten.

The classroom grew still. Hobie thought about the Japanese kids who'd been at their school. One day they were there, and the next day they weren't. They'd been sent away to camps because of Pearl

Harbor. Hobie didn't even know where Tomiko went. Maybe to Minidoka. That's where Uncle Tryg's neighbors, the Sasakis, were. And from *their* letters, it didn't sound like those camps were very nice.

"Tomiko was a great jump roper," said Catherine.

"I still have the origami frog she made me," said Marty.

"Remember when she brought us rice-paper candies on her birthday?" asked Preston.

Dorine put her head down. Tears dribbled onto her desk. Mrs. Thornton placed her arm around Dorine's quaking shoulders.

"Thank you, dear, for helping us remember a good friend," she said.

After a few moments, Dorine lifted her head up. Mrs. Thornton whispered something in her ear. Dorine nodded and left the room.

Mrs. Thornton went back to the front, by her desk. "Hobie, would you like to go next?"

Hobie stood up, his notes in hand. "I have a German shepherd, Duke. He's really smart. And fast. And brave."

He caught Mitch's eye as he said this. "Well, my neighbor told me that the Army needed dogs. And then I heard about some kids on the Hop Harrigan show who gave their dog to the Army. And, well, I know how important it is to give our all here at home —" That earned a nod from Mrs. Thornton. Hobie stood taller.

"So I *loaned* Duke to the Dogs for Defense." He set down his notes to pick up the encyclopedia. "This is a picture of a German shepherd." He turned the page. "And this is a Doberman pinscher. Those are two of the Army's favorite dogs." He flipped the page again. "But I read a story about a dog like this" — he pointed to a picture of a Scottish terrier — "who's the mascot for an air squadron. His name is Mac and he's logged over two hundred hours of flying time."

"Nifty!" Marty exclaimed.

"Some of the dogs were trained to guard places like Boeing —"

Marty interrupted. "There's a dog named Sparky that my dad sees when he works the night shift."

Mrs. Thornton pursed her lips. "That's a wonderful contribution, Marty. But do wait your turn, please."

"Sorry." Marty ducked his head.

Hobie continued. "Like I said, some dogs stayed here. But Duke got placed with the Marines. His handler, Private Marvin Corff, wrote me that they've finished their training at Camp Lejeune and are heading for California." Hobie paused to catch his breath. "So that's about it on Dogs for Defense."

"I think it's wonderful, what you're doing for the Marines." Mrs. Thornton used her handkerchief again.

"Well, Duke's doing the work, not me." Hobie folded his notes back up and slipped them in his pocket. "But I'm glad he's in California. Not in the war somewhere."

"Maybe you could bring him to school when he comes back," Catherine suggested.

"Dogs are not generally allowed at school," said Mrs. Thornton.

The class groaned its disappointment.

Mrs. Thornton held up her hand. "But I would imagine exceptions could be made for war heroes."

"Oh, goody!" Millie Swenson and two other girls jumped up and down in their seats.

Hobie sat down. Very fast.

He was even more embarrassed at lunch, when Catherine walked up to where he was sitting at the boys' table and whapped him on the shoulder. "I'm not mad at you anymore for giving Duke away," she said. "It was really brave."

"Stupid's more like it," Mitch said.

"Oh, grow up, Mitch." Catherine made a face at him, then stomped off to the girls' table.

Mitch speared a canned peach slice with his fork. "At least I know what it means when a Marine is sent to California."

Hobie folded the flaps back on his milk carton. "What are you talking about?"

Mitch said one word, "Pacific."

"What?" Hobie stopped in mid-fold.

"California means one thing." Mitch slurp-swallowed the peach. "They're headed for the Pacific. One of those islands that isn't even a dot on the globe." He waved a hand vaguely. "Guam. Tarawa. Something like that."

An ache started deep in Hobie's stomach. Only the night before, he'd seen a headline on the front page of the *Seattle Daily Times*, about the Marines "carrying the fight" to the Japanese on Tarawa and Truk islands.

"You don't know that," Max said. He turned toward Hobie. "Don't listen to him," he said.

Hobie caught Preston's eye across the table. "Is Mitch right? Do you think they're going there?"

Preston ducked his head, but before he could say anything, Mitch answered. "They're Marines," he said, as if that explained everything.

Hobie pushed the milk carton away, sick because he knew Mitch was right. Now, because of what *he'd* done, Duke was going to be in the war. Fighting! In the Pacific! Why had he listened to Mr. Gilbert? Mr. Rasmussen? Why had he fallen for all that business about doing his part, being a good home-front soldier?

Hobie didn't hear much of anything else the rest of the day. June had Brownies, so he walked home by himself. The soles of his shoes slapped out a rhythm against the pavement. *Dumb, dumb, dumb.*

How could he have done that to Duke? His best friend. Duke would have done anything to protect Hobie, to keep him safe. Hobie was such a lousy friend; he not only didn't keep Duke safe, he put him in danger.

Hobie was mad enough to throw a rock through Mr. Rasmussen's window. Lots of rocks.

Not that he'd really do it, but it felt awfully good to think about it. Hobie bent down to pick one up. Next to it was a penny. Heads' side up. "Find a penny, pick it up. All day long, you'll have good luck."

Hobie put the penny in his pocket. He could use some good luck.

Because no matter what, Duke was not going to war.

Hobie was going to get him home.

CHAPTER ELEVEN

No More Pencils, No More Books!

June 16, 1944

With a lacy handkerchief pressed to her nose, Mrs. Thornton bid her fifth graders farewell. "I will never forget any of you," she said. "Please come see me next year." She was so sincere that even Ervin Malk, who'd never turned in a lick of schoolwork, said he would.

"Maybe I'll see you at the playfield," Catherine said to Hobie as he gathered his gear from the cloakroom. "We could play baseball."

"If I'm not helping my uncle, that'd be great," Hobie said.

"It's a deal!" Catherine punched him on the arm. "See you around, Hobie! You, too, Max." Max wasn't quick enough to sidestep Catherine's punch, either.

"She's strong for a girl," Max said, rubbing his arm.

"She's strong period," said Hobie. "See you later, Max."

June was in especially high spirits. "Look!" She showed Hobie a big blue ribbon, imprinted with gold: *First Grade Top Speller*. "Miriam got one just like it," she said. "Teacher said it's the first time there's ever been a tie."

Hobie could smell chocolate cake half a block from home.

June picked up the scent, too. "Red Velvet!" she said, skipping ahead.

And she was right.

"I had enough sugar ration points for an end-of-the-school-year cake," Mom said.

Hobie stuck his finger in the mixing bowl. Mom's special fudge frosting!

"Can we have a piece right now?" June asked.

Mom clucked her tongue. "No, you may not, silly goose." She gave the frosting another stir, plopped some on top of the cake, and began to spread it around. "I invited Auntie Ellen and the boys for dinner. We'll celebrate with them."

"Mo-ommy!" June flopped onto a kitchen chair. "No fair."

Mom held up the frosting-covered spatula and pointed to the sampler on the kitchen wall. The one that said, *Friends double our joys and halve our sorrows.*

"That's about friends." June rested her cheek on the tabletop. "Not relatives."

Mom handed the spatula to June. "Do you want to help me frost the cake?"

June perked right up. Hobie breathed in deep of the good chocolate smell. That, and one lousy piece of cake, would be all he'd get once his cousins arrived.

"Did Auntie Ellen say when Uncle Tryg would be back?" Hobie asked. He hadn't forgotten about Dad asking him to help with the boat.

"Sounds like in about two more weeks," Mom said. "The fishing's been pretty good up north."

Hobie couldn't wait to write Dad to tell him how he'd helped on the *Lily Bess*. "Is it okay if I go for a bike ride?" Hobie asked.

"Can we put a candle on the cake?" June asked Mom. "It's Kitty's birthday."

While they rummaged around in drawers, looking for a birthday candle, Hobie took off on his bike. Even though he'd been out of school for less than an hour, he found himself heading back that way.

It turned out he wasn't the only one who wasn't quite ready to leave fifth grade behind. There were about a dozen kids on the playground, circling around Catherine.

"Hey, Hobie." She waved him over. "We're going to play some baseball."

Hobie skidded his bike to a stop, dropping it at the edge of the circle of kids. Catherine picked him for her team, along with Marty and Preston and a couple of fourth-grade girls.

Catherine was kind of bossy, but she could pitch. Besides, it was her ball. Marty brought the bat, and Preston wore a practically brand-new JC Higgins glove on his right hand.

One of the fourth graders stepped up to bat. She was so skinny she could hardly keep the bat off her shoulder.

"Batter-batter-batter," Marty chattered at her from second base.

"Easy out!" called another kid.

Preston stood right on first base, punching his hand into his glove. Hobie could tell Preston would've been a lot happier if they were all in the library, looking something up in the encyclopedia. But he was trying.

Hobie played the field. The entire field. There weren't enough kids for three outfielders. Besides, it was only a pickup game. He didn't imagine he'd get many balls his way. Especially not from this batter.

"Strike one!" the catcher called.

The fourth-grade girl waggled the bat around.

"You can do it, Cookie!" her friend called.

"Yeah, Kooky, you can do it!" Marty hollered.

Cookie stuck her chin out, waiting for Catherine's pitch. She stepped forward and swung.

Thwack! The ball sailed over Catherine's head, straight for Hobie. He poured on the speed to get to the ball, which was dropping, dropping, dropping. He dived, headfirst, arms outstretched, hands cupped up.

The ball bounced behind him.

"Run, Cookie!" her friend yelled. "Run!"

Cookie dropped the bat and ran. She rounded first before Hobie got himself upright and grabbed the ball. She was safe at second.

Hobie tossed the ball to Catherine. "Sorry," he said.

"For what?" Catherine slapped the ball into her glove. "This is only a game!"

Cookie hopped up and down like second base was a trampoline. "I did it!" she called.

Hobie jogged back out to the field. While he was standing there, waiting for Catherine to pitch to Cookie's friend, he saw Max ride by on his bike. Hobie waved at him and Max waved back. He had a canvas shopping bag slung over his back. Hobie hoped that didn't mean more pigs' feet.

Cookie's friend struck out, and so did the next batter.

Catherine and Marty got hits when it was their ups, but neither scored. After a few more innings, Catherine's mother pulled up to the curb and tapped on the horn of their DeSoto.

"I have to go," Catherine said. "Sorry." The other pitcher handed her the ball, and they shook hands. "We should do this again," Catherine called as she jogged for the car. "Bye!"

Kids started heading for home. Hobie wiped his

sweaty face, then got a long drink at the drinking fountain.

"See you around," he called to Marty and Preston. They were headed in the opposite direction.

As he rode home, Hobie realized he'd been so busy with baseball, he hadn't given one thought to how he was going to get Duke home. He thought about a comment Mrs. Thornton had written on his report card: *Hobie is an excellent problem solver.*

He stood up on his pedals and coasted a ways. If Mrs. Thornton said it, it must be so.

He turned up his street. There were cousins and chocolate cake waiting.

There was always tomorrow to hatch a new plan.

CHAPTER TWELVE

Fielder's Choice

June 30, 1944

Hobie tucked a peanut butter sandwich inside his baseball glove and hung it from the handlebars. Nearly every day, after weeding and watering the Victory garden, he'd ridden his bike to the school. And every day there was a bunch of kids gathered, ready to play ball. Sometimes they hit around until there were enough for two teams. Then they played until three, when the guys with paper routes had to leave to pick up their papers.

Hobie wasn't sure how many more ball games he could make. Uncle Tryg was due home within the week, and who knew how much help he'd want with the *Lily Bess*. Dad's last letter had included a list of ways Hobie could pitch in. *Don't wait for Tryg to ask you to do something*, he'd written. *If you see a job to do, do it.* Hobie hoped he wouldn't let Dad — or Uncle Tryg — down.

Riding to the school yard, Hobie wondered if

they'd have enough for two teams today. The teams shifted around a bit depending on who showed up, but Catherine was always one of the captains. She brought the baseball. And she usually picked Hobie for her team.

Hobie counted heads as he coasted across the school yard to the backstop. Fifteen already! Enough for two teams.

Cookie and her friend Nina showed up with a bunch of other kids from their grade.

"We should play fourth against fifth," Marty suggested.

"You mean fifth against sixth," Catherine corrected. "We're officially sixth graders now."

"Right." Marty tapped the side of his head. "In the summer, I block school stuff out of my brain!"

"Me, too," said the other captain, Mike Feeney.

"Not me," said Preston Crane. "I miss school."

"You would," Marty groaned. "Let's just play ball."

They divvied up the teams into the two grades and played all morning.

The almost-sixth graders beat the almost-fifth graders, but only by a run.

"Let's take a lunch break." Marty plunked down on the grass. "I'm starving."

"Glad to meet you, Starving," said Hobie.

"Very funny." Marty flopped onto his back. "I'm thirsty, too. Anyone else want to ride over to Lee's for a soda?"

The other kids were fine with the water fountain, so it was just Hobie and Marty who went to Lee's. Hobie had a dime. He picked out a grape soda for himself.

"Do you think Catherine would rather have grape or root beer?" Hobie asked Marty. Since Catherine brought the ball every day, he thought she deserved a soda, too.

"Root beer." Marty picked out a Bubble Up for himself. "Hey, you want to come over later? Listen to *Hop Harrigan* with me?"

"Sure!" Hobie thought about all the times he and Scooter had sat in Hobie's kitchen, waiting to hear what Hop was going to do that day. If the story was a dud, Scooter added his own sound effects. And not always polite ones. But Hobie laughed, no matter what.

Mrs. Lee took their change. "No joke today?" she asked.

Hobie thought for a second. What was the one he'd just read? "Okay. What do you get when you cross a sheepdog with a rose?"

Mrs. Lee wrinkled up her forehead, thinking. Marty did, too.

"I give," Marty said, popping the cap off his soda bottle.

"Some kind of flower?" Mrs. Lee guessed.

Hobie grinned. "A *collie*-flower."

She shook her head. Marty coughed on his drink.

"I didn't say it was a good joke," Hobie said.

"Any joke is a good joke," Mrs. Lee declared. "A daily chuckle is as good as vitamins."

As they headed out the door, Max was coming in, working hard on a piece of gum.

"Hi!" Hobie hadn't really seen Max, except for when he rode by the school yard every now and again.

Max blew a black bubble. Black Jack gum. The same kind Hobie liked. "What are you guys doing?"

"Playing baseball over at the school," Marty answered.

Hobie remembered seeing a baseball mitt hanging off Max's bike once. "Do you want to come?"

Max shrugged. "I don't know." But he sounded like he did know.

"Go along," Mrs. Lee said. "It'd be good for you."

"We could use another guy," said Marty.

"Okay." Max pulled a shopping list from his pocket. "As soon as I take these things home to Ma, I'll be over."

"See you soon," Hobie said.

Back at the school yard, he opened the soda bottles on his belt buckle, then handed Catherine the root beer.

"Wow, thanks." She took a big swallow. "My favorite."

Marty elbowed Hobie. "Told you," he said.

"We ran into Max," Hobie said. "He might be coming over."

"Dibs!" Catherine said. "Besides, that'll even up the teams."

The other captain spit in the dirt at her feet. "We're still going to beat you."

"Says who?" Catherine let go with a prodigious belch for emphasis.

"Catherine!" Cookie giggled. "That's not very ladylike."

Catherine answered with another belch.

That led to a burping contest that Marty easily won.

"Bubble Up," he told Catherine, letting her in on his trade secret. "Works every time."

"Ready to go?" asked the other captain.

"Max isn't here yet," Catherine said.

"We should probably start without him," said Marty. "In case he can't come."

"Let's wait a few more minutes," suggested Hobie. He threw the wax paper wrapper from his sandwich into the garbage. "There he is!"

Max cycled toward them, cheeks red. "I got here as fast as I could," he gasped.

"Let's go." Catherine held a bat out to the other captain. He gripped it with one hand, and she snugged her hand next to his. They went back and forth like that until they ran out of bat. Catherine's hand was on top.

"We choose last ups," she said.

Max joined Hobie in the field.

The score went back and forth, back and forth.

But in the top of the ninth, their team was ahead by one run. With two outs, Cookie stepped up to bat.

"Batter can't hit!" Marty hollered.

Hobie looked over at Max. "Yes, she can," he said. "Heads up!"

Max pounded his fist into his glove, crouching down to the ready position.

"What's that out in the field?" a familiar voice hollered. "Not a pair of dice, but a pair of dunces."

Mitch Mitchell strolled up behind the backstop, flanked by a couple of seventh graders Hobie had seen around.

"That's so funny, I forgot to laugh," Catherine said.

"Don't listen to him," Marty called over his shoulder to Max and Hobie.

Max eased up out of his crouch.

"Marty's right," Hobie called. "Let's keep our heads in the game."

Mitch kept at it with the snide comments. "Go ahead," he said to Cookie. "Hit it a good one. They can't catch it."

Catherine wound up and delivered her pitch.

"Strike one!" called the catcher.

Cookie stamped her foot. "Darn it," she said. She lifted the bat to her shoulder.

"It's not fielder's choice, but fielder's chumps!" Mitch howled at his own bad joke.

Hobie punched his fist into his glove.

Catherine released the ball.

"Strike two!"

"You can do it, Cookie!" her teammates called.

Cookie held up her hand, to indicate time. Then she turned to face Mitch. Hobie had no idea what she said, but whatever it was, it shut Mitch up.

Cookie stepped back up to the plate.

She swung.

She connected.

"Easy score!" Mitch shouted.

"Mine!" Max yelled, running in on the ball. Then it seemed to shift course, looking to fall right behind him. Max pivoted and dived.

"He got it!" Hobie shouted. "He got it!"

Max leaped up, holding the gloved ball high.

"Yippee ki yi!" screamed Catherine.

Marty put his fingers in his mouth and whistled.

"That was beautiful," Hobie said. "How did you do it?"

Max tossed the ball back to Catherine. "Beginner's luck," he said. "The first ball I've ever caught."

"Well, keep it up!" said Hobie.

Max brushed the knees of his dungarees.

"You're bleeding," Hobie said.

"And it stings like heck, too!" Max looked at his elbows, then back at Hobie like the cat that caught the canary. "It was worth it, just to shut Mitch up."

They jogged in to congratulate Catherine.

"I wish I had a camera," she said.

"Yeah, that was some catch," Hobie said.

"Not for that." She covered a smile with her hand. "For the look on Mitch's face!" She blew a raspberry at Mitch's departing back.

Max turned to Hobie. "Do you want to come over today?" he asked.

Marty ran up and punched Hobie on the arm. "Ready to listen to *Hop Harrigan*?"

"Sorry, Max. Another time!" Hobie followed Marty to grab their bikes. "Good game, everybody!"

Catherine gave Hobie a funny look. "What?" he asked her.

She kept glaring.

Girls.

Max hooked his glove over his handlebar. "Bye, Catherine," he said.

"See you, Max!" Hobie called.

But Max must not have heard him because he didn't answer.

"Come on!" Marty called. "The show might be starting." He raced away from the school yard.

"Wait up!" Hobie pedaled after Marty, so fast he was nearly flying.

Hobie Hanson, Ace of the Airways.

CHAPTER THIRTEEN

A Doggone Day

July 5, 1944

Hobie groaned as he rolled over. Maybe he shouldn't have eaten that fourth hot dog last night. That would teach him to take a dare from Erik.

He pushed himself out of bed, threw on some clothes, and went to the kitchen.

"Ouch, Mommy!" June squirmed as Mom dabbed Unguentine on her sunburned shoulders.

"This will help it feel better," Mom assured her. "Now sit still."

June fussed but let Mom finish applying a layer of the stuff.

"Your face looks a little pink, too." Mom motioned Hobie over and smeared some ointment on his nose. "I guess we all got too much sun at the picnic yesterday."

Hobie poured a glass of milk. "I think I'll just have a piece of toast for breakfast," he said.

June pretended to feed Kitty some cereal. "What

was your favorite part of the picnic, Kitty? I liked wading in the lake." She listened to her doll. "Oh, the ice cream was good, too." June munched a spoonful of cereal. "What was your favorite part, Mommy?"

Mom poured herself a cup of coffee. "Being with family. It's so nice for Ellen and the boys that Tryg is home."

"Uncle Tryg's the best hot dog roaster in the world!" June exclaimed.

Hobie groaned again. "Do not mention hot dogs." He set down his toast.

"What was your favorite part?" June asked. "Probably the fireworks."

"Those were nifty, but when that B-29 flew over, that was something! It made those B-17s look like toys."

As part of the city's celebration, there'd been a flyover. One of Boeing's brand-new B-29s and two B-17s. The noise of that big plane, the Superfortress, had drilled right down into Hobie's bones. Erik and Emil had even stopped their usual clowning around to watch. He wondered again, as he had last night, what Dad had done to celebrate Independence Day.

Maybe he got in another mission. One mission closer to coming home.

"After breakfast, can you run to Lee's for me? We're out of condensed milk," Mom said. "Did Uncle Tryg need you today?"

Hobie drained his glass. "No. He said tomorrow or the next day; he had some stuff he needed to do around the house first."

"Then you'll have time to mow the lawn," Mom said.

Across the room, the Kit-Cat clock, eyes moving and tail twitching, showed nine. If Hobie hustled to the store, he could mow and still make it to the school for baseball.

He ate the last bites of his toast. "I'll be back soon," he said. He quickly brushed his teeth, and then zoomed over to Lee's.

Mrs. Lee was helping a lady when he got there. He had to wait his turn while they discussed which soap flakes were the best buy. The lady finally decided on Lux.

"Oh, don't go yet, Edna," Mrs. Lee said. "I bet Hobie's got a joke for us."

Hobie felt a little odd telling a joke to a stranger, but he went ahead. "Dad sent me this in his last letter," he said. "What do you get if you cross a skunk and a dog?"

"Tomato juice," said the lady. "That's the only thing that gets out the skunk smell."

"Right, but this is a joke, Edna." Mrs. Lee pursed her lips. "I give!"

"Rid of the dog," Hobie said.

The lady, Edna, hooted with laughter. "I'm going to tell that to my grandson. If I can remember it!" As she walked out of the store, Hobie heard her muttering, "Cross a skunk and a dog. Skunk and dog."

"Oh, that was one of your best." Mrs. Lee was still chuckling as Hobie handed over the ration stamps and twenty-nine cents for the two tins of milk.

The dog joke reminded Hobie that he still hadn't come up with a solution for getting Duke back. And there'd been another letter from Pfc. Corff. This time, he'd tucked in a few photos of him and Duke, with some of the other war dogs.

He pedaled home, thinking hard. Could he talk Mom into taking a vacation to California? Then they could bring Duke back. Hobie jounced over a crack in the sidewalk. Not likely. Even if Mom liked to drive long distances, which she didn't, there was the little problem of gas rationing.

Hobie concentrated so hard on getting Duke back, he could almost hear him.

Hobie cocked his head.

He *did* hear a dog. Whimpering.

Hobie veered around. The sound seemed to be coming from a shed on the vacant lot behind him.

He eased closer. A kid knelt on the floor of the shed, his back to Hobie. The dog — some kind of black-and-white mutt — was on the ground. A string of tin cans was tied to its tail.

"Hey," Hobie said, stepping forward. "Leave that poor dog alone." He jerked the boy's shoulder.

It was Max.

"What are you doing?" Hobie couldn't believe Max would be so cruel.

"I didn't do this," Max said. "I'm trying to *undo* it." He pulled out a pocketknife to cut through the twine. "Geez. This is tied so tight, I'm afraid I'm going to cut him."

The dog thrashed wildly to get away from Max and his knife. But it didn't growl or try to bite.

"Let me help." Hobie knelt down. The dog looked like some kind of lab but with shorter legs. "Hey there, boy —" He did a quick check. "I mean, girl. It's okay. We won't hurt you."

She twisted around again, trying to get free. Hobie began stroking the spot between her eyes. That used to calm Duke down when he was riled up.

"Let's get those dumb cans off you, okay?" Hobie spoke calmly. Quietly. After a few more minutes, the dog stopped squirming. She rolled on her back. "Good girl," Hobie said, rubbing her skinny belly.

Max quickly sliced the string to free the cans. "I need to get that part off her tail. It's so tight, she's bleeding."

Hobie could see he was right. "I don't suppose you have any food on you?"

Max shook his head.

"Me, either." It was going to be tricky. Without a treat to distract her, how were they going to cut that string? Hobie thought about the first time he'd had to trim Duke's toenails. Man, did Duke put up a fight! Then Hobie got the idea to leave the trimmers around, by Duke's dish, by his blanket in the kitchen, in Hobie's room. He gave Duke every chance to check them out. And he praised Duke every time he let Hobie touch him with the trimmers. It took a while, but Duke got used to them.

"Let her sniff the knife," Hobie told Max.

"What?" Max asked.

"Just try it."

Max held out the knife while Hobie kept petting the dog. Praising her.

"See? That won't hurt you," Hobie said as she nosed at the knife handle. He rub-rub-rubbed her belly.

"We need to use it, to get the string off," he explained to the dog. He could feel her relax under his petting and words. After a while, he motioned for Max to cut.

"Got it!" Max said, holding up the snipped string. "Wow, you're good with dogs."

"Well, I have one, you know." The words slipped out before Hobie could stop them. But he did have a dog. And would have him back soon.

Max reached over and began petting the dog's head. She kept trying to lick him. "I bet she got scared by the fireworks last night and ran away," he said.

"Maybe," said Hobie. "But her ribs are poking out, and" — he waved his hand in front of his nose — "she stinks." He saw something jump in her fur. "Looks like fleas, too."

"One of us needs to take her home." Max stroked her silky black ears. "I mean, while we look for her family."

The dog barked. "She likes that idea." Max scratched her under the chin.

"I have all the dog stuff," Hobie said. "I bet Mom would say okay to keeping her for a while."

Max ducked his head. "I know you're good with dogs," he said. "But I'd like to take her." He pulled a twig off the dog's fur.

"Sure. Go ahead," Hobie said.

Max rocked back on his heels. "The thing is, Ma says we don't need another mouth to feed."

"I can bring over some of Duke's food," Hobie offered. "And you could tell your mom it probably wouldn't be for very long. I'll help you put up signs."

Max rubbed the dog's head. "Yeah. Not for very long." But he didn't sound happy about that.

"We can start on the signs this afternoon," Hobie said. "I gotta mow the lawn first." He could skip the baseball game this once. For a good cause.

"Okay." Max stared into the dog's face. "For now, I'll call you Pepper," he said.

Hobie's neck was itchy from mowing the grass. He turned on the kitchen faucet and ducked his head under it. He felt even better after downing an ice-cold glass of lemonade.

"Someone's at the door!" June called.

"I'll get it." Hobie scrambled to beat his sister to answer it.

It was Max. "I hope it's okay that I brought Pepper," Max said. "By the way, did you know you have some mail?"

"Did you get a dog?" June pushed under Hobie's arm. "Here, doggy."

"She's lost," Hobie said, reaching around through the doorjamb to pull the letters from their mailbox.

"But I'm keeping her while we look for the owners," Max explained. "Hey, one of those letters is to you."

The top envelope was addressed to Hobie. In Pfc. Corff's handwriting.

"It's from Duke!" June exclaimed. "Read it!"

"Duke?" Max said. "Isn't that your dog?"

"Uh, yeah." Hobie cleared his throat. "His handler writes me like Duke's writing." Would Max laugh at him? Call him a baby?

Max tilted his head. "Wow. That's nifty."

Hobie let out the breath he realized he'd been holding. "Do you want to hear it?"

"Yes!" June and Max said at the same time. June scooted onto the porch swing. "Here, Pepper."

Pepper looked at Max. "It's okay, girl," he said. Pepper jumped up next to June as Max leaned against the railing.

Hobie opened the envelope and began to read.

Dear Hobie,

The war dogs unit is in tip-top shape, even if the two-legged Marines don't have quite the pep that my four-legged buddies and I do.

You'll be glad to know that I passed my swimming test with flying colors. I can dog-paddle with the best of them!

We're at a new camp now. Not posh by a long shot, but I get to bunk with Marv, so that's okay. It's kind of hot where we are. Times like this, I almost wish I was a Doberman. Less fur.

Time for chow.

Your pal,

Duke

P.S. Duke has been swell; he is one of the top dogs in the unit. Bet you're not surprised about that. I sure sleep better at night now. I'd take him over Rin Tin Tin any day.

Semper Fi,

Marv

June clapped her hands when Hobie finished. "I knew Duke would be the best dog," she said.

Hobie flicked his finger against the corner of the letter. He didn't feel like talking for a minute.

Max looked at him. "It sounds like Duke's doing great," he said. "Like they're both doing great."

Hobie slowly folded up the letter. What it sounded like was that Pfc. Corff and Duke were becoming best friends.

"Even if he's in the Marines, he's still your dog," Max said, as if he could read Hobie's mind.

"I know," Hobie said. But a little seed of doubt had been planted. "Well, we better get to work on those signs."

Max moved toward the open door and Pepper jumped off the swing to follow.

"Do you want to help us?" Max asked June.

"No!" said Hobie.

"Yes!" June slid off the swing. "We can use my new crayons."

Hobie made a face. "She's never going to leave us alone," he warned.

Max jiggled the rope leash he'd rigged up. "Sorry."

An only child like Max probably didn't understand anything about little sisters. Hobie sighed. "It's okay."

They scrounged up some blank paper and went to work. Pepper plunked down on the floor under the kitchen table.

"I'm doing my best penmanship," June said. "Isn't it good, Max?"

"Very nice." Max looked up from the sign he was working on. "I like the colors you chose, too."

June began to sing. "How much is that doggy in the window? The one with the waggledy tail? How much is that doggy in the window? I do hope that doggy's for sale!"

Pepper's tail thumped on the floor.

"She likes my song!" June said.

Hobie was almost finished with the sign he was working on. "What's your telephone number?" he asked Max.

"Aren't I a good singer?" June said, coloring in the picture of a dog she'd drawn. "Aren't I?"

"Real good," Max said to her. Then he gave his number to Hobie.

Mom brought them some cookies as they finished up.

"Ten, eleven, twelve." Hobie counted the signs. "This should get us started anyway. Are you ready?"

"Can I come?" June asked.

Hobie answered before Max could. "No."

"Mommy!" June whined.

Mom popped her head in the kitchen. "June, the boys don't need you tagging along today. Why don't you help me pick some peas for dinner?"

"I'd rather go with them." June pointed at the boys. "I could hold on to Pepper."

"June." Mom used her that's-the-end-of-the-discussion voice. "Come with me."

Max tugged on Pepper's leash. "Let's go, girl." Neither he nor Pepper seemed too excited.

"I thought we'd hang a couple by where we found her," Hobie said.

Max clumped down the steps. Slowly. "Okay. And I guess we should hang a couple near the school."

"Maybe Mrs. Lee would let us hang one up at her store," Hobie suggested.

They figured out twelve places to hang the signs, saving Lee's Grocery for last.

"Here," said Max, handing Hobie the leash. "You watch Pepper while I go in and ask."

Hobie scratched Pepper's back. He could see that Max was getting very attached to her. That would only make it harder to give her up to her real family.

"She said okay." Max jumped down the steps. "But she said she hadn't heard of anyone losing a dog lately." He rubbed Pepper's head. "Maybe you don't have a family," he said. "Yet."

One look at Max's face and Hobie knew he had fallen for Pepper, hook, line, and sinker.

CHAPTER FOURTEEN

News

July 20, 1944

Hobie took the steel brush and sandpaper from Uncle Tryg.

"You can use the paper wet or dry," Uncle Tryg explained. "But we need to get every bit of rust off that anchor." He chuckled. "I guess I don't mean 'we' — I mean 'you.' I'll be working on the engine. You okay here?"

Hobie took one look at the anchor braced up on the sawhorses. Even though he wasn't sure he was okay, he told Uncle Tryg that he was. He set the supplies on the deck and inspected the anchor more closely. He was going to grow some muscles scraping away all that rust, no doubt about it. He arranged a canvas tarp under the anchor and got to work.

At noon, Uncle Tryg announced a lunch break. "I'm not done yet," Hobie said.

Uncle Tryg's laugh bubbled up from his toes. "And you won't be done for a goodly while," he said. "All the more reason to stop for lunch."

They ate the sandwiches Aunt Ellen had made, watching the boats moving about in the harbor. "Doesn't it make you want to go somewhere?" Uncle Tryg asked Hobie.

Hobie didn't answer. He liked being right where he was. He didn't really want to go anywhere else. He just wanted the ones he cared about — Dad and Duke — to come here. Come home.

Uncle Tryg chewed up the last of his sandwich, washing it down with a swig of coffee.

"Best get back at it." He and Hobie worked for another couple of hours. Hobie sanded and scrubbed until his arms burned. He'd barely made a dent in the rust. He sat back on his haunches, wiping sweat from his forehead with the hem of his T-shirt.

Uncle Tryg tapped him on the shoulder. "Stow your supplies," he said. "I've got chores at home." Uncle Tryg picked up his lunch pail and thermos. "Can I drop you somewhere?"

"Sure." It'd been a few days since Hobie had been able to check in on Max and Pepper, see how they were doing with the obedience training. "My friend's house."

Hobie stashed the sandpaper and brushes in a footlocker. He rolled his bike down the dock to Uncle Tryg's car and lifted it into the trunk.

Uncle Tryg told Hobie about the letter they'd gotten from Erik and Emil, who were at Bible camp for two weeks. "Those two knuckleheads get themselves into more trouble," he said. "They got the brainy idea to stick all of their counselor's socks in the camp freezer!" He sounded cross, but his eyes were twinkling.

"That's the house there." Hobie pointed at the Kleins'.

Uncle Tryg pulled up to the curb and then unlocked the trunk.

"Same time tomorrow morning?" Hobie lifted out his bike.

"That'll be fine." Uncle Tryg winked at Hobie. "Now, no turning your sister's socks into Popsicles," he said.

"I wouldn't dream of it!" Hobie straightened the front wheel to get the bike rolling. "Our icebox doesn't even have a freezer," he added.

Uncle Tryg burst out laughing. "See you tomorrow, son." He drove off.

Hobie followed the barking to the backyard. It'd been two weeks since Max had found Pepper. Two weeks and over two dozen "found dog" signs. But no one had telephoned to claim her.

"Which one of you is getting the bath?" Hobie asked. Both Max and Pepper were soaking.

"It's supposed to be her," Max said. He squirted more Magi-Tex pet shampoo on Pepper's back. He and Hobie had each chipped in thirty cents to buy the shampoo at Bartell's. Hobie dropped his bike and went over to help scrub. "Hey, Pepper. Hey, girl." He rubbed shampoo down her hind legs.

Pepper's coat had grown in shiny black. Not one flea floated in the washtub today. She'd put on some weight, too.

Max hosed off the lather. "Better duck!" he hollered. They were too slow. Pepper shook herself all over, nailing them but good. Hobie wiped his face, sputtering. Max finished rinsing her. "You're not a nuisance, are you, girl?"

Pepper tried to lap at the water pouring from the hose.

"Ma says she can stay another week and that's it." Max stared off into space, water cascading on his sneakers. "Then it's the pound." Hobie swallowed hard. The pound would only keep a dog for a week or two. Then it was all over.

Hobie turned off the faucet. "We'll think of something," he said. "I know we will."

Max dropped the hose. "I sure hope so." Pepper jumped out of the washtub and ran around the yard, rolling on the grass.

"She's happy that June's not here," Hobie said. The last time June had come over, they'd caught her trying to dress Pepper up in a skirt and baby bonnet.

Max screwed the lid back on the shampoo bottle. "Yeah," he agreed. "Pepper's not crazy about playing dress-up."

Pepper heard her name and trotted up to Max. He stroked her wet head.

"What are we going to do, Pep?" he asked. Her answer was to take off again, running and rolling. "That is one goofy dog," Max said, shaking his head. But Hobie could tell that he didn't really mean it.

"I better get home," Hobie said. Going to work for Uncle Tryg hadn't put a dent in the list of chores Mom made for him each day. "See you tomorrow?"

"Sure." Max grabbed Pepper as she ran by, and buckled her collar back on. "Give me a call if you get any brilliant ideas."

Hobie thought hard all the way home. He'd already asked Mrs. Lee if she'd like a dog, seeing as she was so fond of jokes about them. But she worried that Pepper was too peppy. She had promised to see if any of her customers might be able to take her home. So far, no one had said yes.

Hobie even asked Aunt Ellen, but she only rolled her eyes. "I have two wild animals already," she said. "I can't handle one more."

Hobie and Max were running out of options. The only other thing Hobie could think of was for them to take Pepper and sit outside someplace busy, like the Roxy Theater, and ask people if they wanted a dog as they came out of the show. It might work. Especially if the show was something like *Call of the Wild*. Or *Lassie Come Home*.

As Hobie turned the corner, a Western Union messenger on a bicycle was pedaling from the opposite direction down their street. Hobie's heart dive-bombed his stomach when the messenger dropped his bike on the sidewalk in front of their house. The last telegram they got was when Grandfather Hanson died. Telegrams brought bad news. Hobie tried to run, but his legs had turned to mush. By the time he reached their front walk, the messenger was cycling away.

Mom hadn't seen him yet. She opened the telegram and then felt behind her, collapsing on the porch swing.

"Mom?" Hobie's legs finally started to work again. He pounded up the steps.

She held up the piece of paper. Her mouth opened but no words, no sounds came out.

June came through the front door right then. "Mommy?" she asked. "Mommy?" She crawled up on Mom's lap.

Hobie peered around his sister to see for himself what the telegram said.

The words hit him like a rogue wave.

REPORT JUST RECEIVED THROUGH THE INTERNATIONAL RED CROSS

STATES THAT YOUR HUSBAND SECOND LIEUTENANT PALMER B HANSON IS A PRISONER OF WAR OF THE GERMAN GOVERNMENT LETTER OF INFORMATION FOLLOWS FROM PROVOST MARSHALL GENERAL = J A ULIO THE ADJUTANT GENERAL.

Hobie didn't move. Couldn't move. A picture flashed through his mind of the B-24 model on the floor of the classroom that day. Did Dad's plane crash? Was he hurt? What did it mean to be a prisoner of war? He'd read and heard awful things about the Nazis. What would they do to Dad?

A hundred questions bubbled up inside, but one look at Mom told him not to ask them. Not now.

"Mommy, Mommy." June tugged at Mom's dress.

Mom hugged her close. "It'll be okay, Junebug. Let me catch my breath."

Hobie was too big for such coddling. He wished he wasn't.

"Why are you so sad?" June asked. She stroked Mom's cheek. Mom took her hand and kissed it.

Mom inhaled a shaky breath and looked at Hobie. "Can you play a game or something with June?" she asked. "I should call Tryg." She gave June another squeeze. "Hop down, sweetie."

"I don't want to play a game," June said.

"Then we'll do something else," Hobie told her. He was the man of the house. And Mom needed his help.

But she merely sat there, her left hand holding the telegram and her right hand patting June.

Then she reached out to Hobie, pulling him down next to her. The three of them huddled there, drawing strength and warmth from one another, for a good long while.

Finally, Mom eased June off her lap. "I'd better make that call."

Hobie took June's small hand. "Come on. How about a puzzle?"

"Kitty wants a story," she said.

Hobie hadn't even finished reading the first chapter in *Little House on the Prairie* when Uncle Tryg, Aunt Ellen, and the cousins arrived.

"Palmer could land a cardboard box," Uncle Tryg said, squeezing Mom's shoulder. "He's fine."

"Of course he is." Aunt Ellen tied on one of Mom's extra aprons. "A tough Norwegian like that?" She clucked her tongue. "Those Germans will rue the day."

Mom nodded numbly. June hung on the hem of her dress.

"What's 'rue'?" June asked.

Mom bent to kiss the top of her head. "Why don't you go play with the boys?"

Aunt Ellen took over the kitchen, making coffee for the grown-ups and Kool-Aid for the kids. She started supper, too. One of Hobie's favorites: Porcupine Meatballs.

Emil and Erik set up the Monopoly board. June picked the yellow token, Emil blue, Erik green, and Hobie picked orange. It was his least favorite color. It didn't matter.

"I dibs banker!" said Emil.

"You were the banker last time," said Erik.

"Was not."

"Were too!"

"Hobie's banker," Uncle Tryg pronounced.

Hobie counted out the play money, and they took turns rolling dice and moving the pieces around the board. But June didn't buy one railroad, which was her favorite thing. And Erik forgot to collect rent from Emil three turns in a row.

The whole evening was like that. People tried to do the usual things: fix dinner, wash dishes, listen to the radio. But Aunt Ellen burned the broccoli and Mom used oil instead of Lux soap on the dishes and when the radio crackled with static, no one got up to adjust it.

After supper, Aunt Ellen telephoned the Red Cross. "They said they can help us find out where Palmer is," she reported. "But it may take some time."

Mom twisted a dish towel in her hands. "I wish I could *do* something," she said.

Hobie's insides felt a lot like that dish towel.

Aunt Ellen hugged her. "You can pray," she said. Then she brushed her hands together. "And we can start assembling a care package for him."

The house was heavy with quiet after Uncle Tryg's family left. June had a tummyache. And then a headache. And then a toothache.

"How about if I lay with you until you fall asleep?" Mom asked her.

June thought that was a good idea. Kitty did, too. The three of them curled up on June's bed.

Hobie went to his own room. He flopped, face-down, on the bed, left arm dangling off the edge, reaching for Duke's warm comfort. *He* had a stomachache, too. Like Mom and June, he was worried about Dad. That was the biggest part of his ache. But the other part was a big ball of mad.

How could this have happened? It wasn't fair. Hobie had done everything to be a good home-front soldier, to do his bit. All the war stamps and scrap drives. He had planted a Victory garden. And Duke! He'd given him away to the Army, for crying out loud. And what good had that done for Dad? Nothing.

It wasn't fair. None of his other friends had fathers in the service. Not Max. Or Preston or Catherine. They got to sit down to dinner with their fathers, every single night.

Hobie tried not to think about all those episodes of *Hop Harrigan* where the Germans beat him up and other stuff. Would Dad be safe? He was tough — Uncle Tryg had said that about a dozen times tonight. But was one Dad tough enough for the whole German Army?

Hobie rolled over on his back, a tear trickling into his ear. He'd thumbtacked the spotter model box top to the ceiling. *THE LIBERATOR!* it blared. Until tonight, he'd liked that red, white, and blue reminder of building the model, and of Dad. Now it only added to his stomachache. He grabbed his pillow, swinging it back and forth until he knocked the darn thing down.

Dad wouldn't want Hobie fussing at Mom the way June was. The man of the house had to be strong. And silent. Sometimes, though, a guy needed to talk to someone. And Duke was the best listener Hobie knew.

But he had tried to get him back. Twice! Pfc. Corff said they were a team — dog and Marine. Without Duke, Pfc. Corff couldn't do his job. And despite everything else, Hobie wanted the Marines out there, fighting the bad guys.

Hobie sat upright on the bed, his pillow pressed to his middle. If he were in a comic book, there'd be a lightbulb over his head.

Pfc. Corff needed a dog. And Pepper needed a home! All he had to do was call Mr. Rasmussen, sign Pepper up, and then the Marines could send Duke back. Pepper was as smart as Duke; not as fast, but definitely as smart. And she'd been easy to train. She could catch up in no time.

It was the perfect solution.

CHAPTER FIFTEEN

Situation Normal, All Fouled Up (SNAFU)

July 21, 1944

Mr. Rasmussen had agreed to come over that evening. Hobie couldn't wait to tell Max the good news, but Mom came down with a sick headache.

He carried some weak tea into her bedroom. "Do you want an aspirin?" He pulled the bottle from his pocket. She took two with sips of the tea.

"I'll be up soon," she said. But she was already back down on the pillow, her face the color of library paste. Hobie tiptoed out of the room and closed the door.

"I want Mommy." June pouted when Hobie tried to pour her a bowl of cereal. "You don't do it right. I like the way Mommy does it." She held up her doll. "So does Kitty."

"Mom doesn't feel good," Hobie explained. "Now, do you want regular milk or magic milk?"

"There's no such thing as magic milk." June smoothed out Kitty's dress.

"Have it your way." Hobie hummed as he pushed down the toaster lever.

"Maybe there could be such a thing." June poked at her dry cereal with her spoon.

Hobie hummed louder.

"Okay, okay!" June held up her bowl. "I want the magic milk."

Hobie made a big production of getting the milk bottle from the icebox and bringing it to the table.

"It doesn't look magic," June said.

Hobie set the bottle on the table, then pretended to take something out of his pocket. "Abracadabra, alla kazam!" He blew on his palm and then made sprinkling motions over the milk.

"Ready?" he said, bottle tipped, ready to pour.

"Ready." June stared intently as the milk glugged from bottle to bowl. She took a taste, smacking her lips. "It tastes a little different," she said.

"The taste isn't the best part." Hobie wagged his finger. "No, sir." He leaned into June. "This milk improves your ability to spell."

June looked at him. "Now you're spoofing me."

"Okay. Don't believe me." He poured himself a bowl of Wheato-Naks, too. "But when Miriam

Bennett wins the second-grade spelling ribbon, don't blame me."

June sighed. But she gobbled up her cereal. She even drank the leftover milk in the bottom of the bowl.

"Want to play Sorry?" Hobie asked.

They set up the board in the front room. After June had sent Hobie back to start for the third time, she looked up at him. "Where's Daddy?"

"I don't know." Hobie needed a one or a two to get off Start. He drew a three.

June drew a seven. "When do you think he'll get out of the war camp?"

"I don't know that, either." Hobie drew again. A four. "Just play the game, okay?"

June grabbed Kitty and held her close. "Do you think he's all right?" Her face was pinched with worry.

Hobie blew out a breath. "He's Dad," Hobie said. "He's fine. Fine." He said it firmly, to convince himself as well as June. "Your turn." He wanted answers to those questions, too. But there was no need to take his frustrations out on his little sister. He let her win that round.

And she won the next three.

After six books, two games of Hide and Go Seek, and lunch, Mom made her way to the kitchen.

"Are you feeling any better?" Hobie asked.

"Some." Mom poured herself a glass of tap water. "The tea and aspirin helped."

This was the second sick headache Mom had gotten since the news about Dad. The past week, Hobie had worked extra hard around the house, even doing the vacuuming. Mom said he didn't have to, but with Dad in the prison camp, that only left one parent. Hobie didn't want to take any chances.

"Would you like some more tea?" Hobie hurried to the sink to fill the kettle.

"That does sound good." Mom pulled out a chair and sat down. "I might even have a piece of toast."

"Let me fix it!" Hobie ran to get the bread. "You just sit there."

"I can butter Mommy's toast," said June. "She likes the way I do it. I get the oleo to all the edges."

Mom stretched her arms out, hugging June to her on one side and Hobie on the other. "I am one lucky mom," she said. "What would I do without you two?"

The Kit-Cat clock *tick-tock*ed, the kettle hummed softly on the stovetop, and the icebox chimed in with its own gurgly tune. The comforting kitchen noises and the comforting warmth of Mom's hug dissolved away at least one layer of Hobie's worries.

"If I'd been feeling better," Mom said, "I'd have told you sooner. But I got some more information from the Red Cross last night, after you two went to bed."

"Do they know where Daddy is?" June fiddled with the buttons on Mom's housecoat.

"Not yet, honey. But they're hopeful it won't be too much longer. But no matter where he's sent, they told me he can get as many letters and packages as we want to send." Mom tapped June's nose with her fingertip. "That means you and I better get ready to whip up some cookies pretty soon."

"Oatmeal raisin!" June said, clapping her hands.

"Does he get to write us?" Hobie couldn't remember when they'd gotten their last letter from Dad.

Mom clucked her tongue. "Well, he's *allowed* to send up to three letters a month." She sighed, then released Hobie as the kettle begin to whistle. "The Red Cross lady said it's up to the camp commander if the letters actually get mailed."

"Daddy will write us!" June said confidently.

"Of course he will," Hobie said. He poured the boiling water in a mug and dunked in a tea bag. "Mom means we might not get them, that's all."

The toast popped up. June carefully spread the oleomargarine to the very edges. Mom took a bite. "Delicious," she said. "Thank you both for a tasty breakfast." She blew on her tea. "I've got some errands to run today. Who wants to come with me?"

"Kitty and I do!" June said.

"I was hoping to go over to Max's," Hobie said. "I mean, if you're feeling good enough for me to go."

"It was just a headache, honey." She hugged him. "Thanks for being such a trooper," she said.

"Can I go to Max's house, too?" June jumped up and down. "Please?" When he had discovered how much she loved them, Opa Klein had taken to keeping a small coffee can of butterscotch drops for June in his shop. "More licorice for me," he'd teased.

Mom made a pretend frowny face. "I thought you and Kitty were coming with me!"

"We can do both," June said. "Can't we, Kitty?"

"I don't know," Mom started. "Hobie's had to take care of you all morning."

"I don't mind," Hobie said. The more the merrier to celebrate the good news about Pepper.

Mom glanced around the kitchen. "Where has the real Hobie gone?" she asked. She smiled. "Okay, you two can be off. Just remember —"

"Use your company manners," said June.

"And don't overstay your welcome," added Hobie.

"I guess you *do* listen to what I say," Mom said. "At least every once in a while."

Mr. Gilbert's cat was stretched across the sidewalk in front of his house and wouldn't budge from his sunning spot. Hobie and June stepped over him.

They were still a few blocks from Max's house when they saw Max, hurrying their way. As he got closer, Hobie could see he was wearing a canvas bag slung across his back.

Hobie waved and hollered. "Are you going to Lee's?" he asked.

"I have a penny in my shoe," June offered. "We could buy some bubble gum."

Max trotted closer. "What did you say?"

Hobie pointed to the bag. "Going to get some groceries?"

"No." Max chomped on a wad of Black Jack gum. "I've got good news."

"Me, too," Hobie said.

Max stopped. "You've heard more about your dad?"

"No. Not that." Hobie tapped his heel on the sidewalk.

"When the Red Cross finds him," June said, "I'm going to send him some cookies. Two kinds."

"Well, you go first, then," said Max.

"I've found the perfect place for Pepper!" Hobie was about ready to explode. "I called Mr. Rasmussen and it's all set."

"Who's Mr. Rasmussen?" Max asked. "Pepper's not his, is she?" His face looked panicky.

"No," said Hobie. "But he does look for dogs."

"I don't get it," Max said.

June tugged on Hobie's T-shirt sleeve and pointed to her untied sneaker.

"He's the man who works with Dogs for Defense." Hobie bent down to tie June's shoe. "Since no one's claimed Pepper, he'll take her. For the Army."

Max's face fell. "You gave away my dog?"

Hobie stammered. "Y-your dog?"

"That's my good news. Ma said I could keep her if I paid for food." Max tugged at the canvas sack. "I got a paper route."

"But I didn't know —" Hobie pressed his hand to his head. He was getting Mom's headache. "I've promised Mr. Rasmussen."

"Something doesn't add up here," Max said. "Why were you so quick to call him?"

"Quick?" Hobie said. "It's been a couple of weeks. You were running out of time."

"But why him?" Max asked.

"The Army needs dogs," Hobie began.

"No!" Max shouted so loud that June jumped. "No. *You* need *your* dog. And you thought you could make a trade. Pepper for Duke."

"Pepper's going away?" June asked. She sat on the ground and pulled her Windbreaker over her head.

"It wasn't like that." Hobie stopped. That wasn't true. It *was* like that. But he'd only been looking at things through his eyes. Not Max's. "I thought —"

"I know what you thought." Max slapped Hobie's explanation away. "Well, I *thought* you were my friend."

He stared hard at Hobie. "I should've known better. It was just because of Pepper. You were never really my friend. You never took my side against Mitch."

June's cries turned to sobs. "I like Pepper," she said, raising a wet face to Hobie.

"I'm sorry —"

"And then you went to Marty's house and left me standing there." Max's voice was cold and flat.

Hobie took June's hand and lifted her up. "I helped you with the lost dog signs. Brought you dog food."

Max tugged on the canvas strap over his shoulder. "That was because of Pepper. Not me." Max stormed off.

"Why is Max so mad?" June wiped her eyes with her sleeves.

"Oh, I don't know." Hobie started for home. But he did know.

"Wait up!" June called, scampering after him.

The way Max told it, it did seem kind of crummy of Hobie. Like being a halfway friend. He didn't mean to treat Max badly. He just didn't think about what he was doing.

Hobie kicked the curb. He had messed up big time.

June tugged on the hem of his shirt. "So does Max get to keep Pepper now?" she asked.

"Yep." Hobie sighed. He was glad for Max, really. If anyone knew what it meant to have a dog, it was Hobie. His throat tightened and it was hard to swallow. He thought about how Duke could catch that darned ball no matter how far Hobie threw it. How his soft breathing helped Hobie get back to sleep after a bad dream. And how he'd jumped on Mitch that day, trying to save him.

Hobie reached the front door before June. He opened it and let her go through.

Just like he had to face the fact that he'd messed up with Max, he also had to face the fact that he wasn't going to get Duke back before the war was over. And if he couldn't get him back, he owed it to him to keep him safe.

Before he dialed up Mr. Rasmussen, Hobie did something he should have done a long time ago. He pulled out a piece of paper and started a letter to Pfc. Corff.

Dear Pfc. Corff, he wrote. *There is something I forgot to tell you. If Duke's ears perk up, watch out. That means trouble is near. I'm telling you this because I want you both to get home safe.*

Over and out,

Hobie Hanson

CHAPTER SIXTEEN

Tidal Wave

August 24, 1944

Hobie rode back from Mrs. Lee's with Mom's groceries. Down the block, he saw Max, a satchel full of newspapers on his back. Pepper tagged along, right next to Max's bike. Like Duke used to. He was too far away for Hobie to call out. In six days, they'd be back at school. In the same classroom. It was going to be a long year.

"Hey, Hobie!" Catherine roller-skated down the street toward him. "We've missed you at the baseball games."

Hobie braked to a stop. "I've been helping my uncle," he explained. "On his fishing boat."

"That sounds fun." Catherine looped around Hobie's bike. "Are you working on Saturday?"

"I don't think so." Mom had a back-to-school shopping trip planned. She'd saved enough shoe ration points for new shoes for both Hobie and June.

"Well, we're getting together for one last game

before school starts next week. It'd be great if you could come." Catherine skated backward. On one foot.

"I'll try," Hobie said.

"And ask Max," Catherine added. "He hasn't been around much, either."

"Well, he's got that paper route." Hobie shifted the groceries on his back.

Catherine did another turn before skating away. "See you Saturday," she called.

Mom was getting the mail as Hobie rode up.

"Anything good?" Hobie called.

She pulled out a tiny piece of mail. "It's from Dad!" she said.

Hobie ran up the steps. It was a postcard. Or *Postkarte*.

Hobie learned another German word, too. *Kriegsgefangenen*. Prisoner of War. That's what was printed across the front of the card.

Mom read it to them right away.

Dear Ruthie,

I am a P. of W. at Stalag Luft 1, in Barth, Germany. This is a camp for officers. Most of us are pilots. I am not hurt and am being treated fairly. My return address is on the front of this card. Get in touch with the local Red Cross agent and find out the details about sending letters, packages, etc. Tell Hobie I've learned some new jokes. Tell Junebug that I'm learning to whittle and I'm making a friend for Kitty. Don't worry about me. Aim, fly, fight! And write!

    Love,

    Palmer

Dad was okay! Hobie had to sit down, he was so relieved. He wasn't hurt. And he was with other pilots.

"Oh," Mom said. "I need to hear that again." And she read it one more time.

Hobie pulled the atlas off the bookshelf. It took him a while, but he found Barth.

"That's pretty far north," Mom said when he showed her. "We better add some woolens to Dad's first care package."

"I want to draw him a picture!" June said. "Of me and Kitty."

"Good idea," Mom said. "Why don't you work on

that while I phone Uncle Tryg?" Mom gave June some paper. "Then I'm going to dial up the Red Cross and find out how to get that picture to your father."

"What do you think Daddy's making for Kitty?" June asked Hobie.

"I don't know." Hobie took one of the pieces of paper Mom brought out.

He picked up a pencil. He put it back down. It had never been hard to write a letter to Dad before. But he had never been a prisoner of war before. Dad said he wasn't hurt. But Hobie knew that there were hurts that didn't cause bruises. Like the mix-up with Max.

Hobie picked up the pencil again. Dad was Dad, right? No matter where he was or what had happened. That thought gave Hobie the confidence to start writing.

Dear Dad,

I looked in the atlas. Barth is almost to Denmark. And right on the sea. Mom said it could be cold there in winter. So she's going to knit you a sweater. Navy blue. She says maybe having that sweater will work like carrying an umbrella so that it won't rain.

I am really glad you aren't hurt. Uncle Tryg said you could land a cardboard box in a hurricane. I feel bad about the Lily Bess, Too, *but good that you are safe. And with other pilots. That way you have lots to talk about.*

I love you,
Hobie

Uncle Tryg's family came over that night and everyone pitched in to put together a care package. Mom tucked in wool socks, Aunt Ellen brought some candy bars, and Uncle Tryg threw in several tins of sardines. Emil and Erik added a deck of cards. June drew a picture. And Hobie tucked in his best joke book.

They got the package taped shut and addressed the way the Red Cross said to.

"I'll take it to the post office tomorrow," Uncle Tryg offered.

"I hope he gets it." Mom sighed. "It's a long ways from here to there and lots of chances for it to get lost."

"Or for someone else to take it," added Aunt Ellen.

"Wait!" June jumped up and ran to the kitchen. She came out carrying a bottle of milk. "Everybody needs a glass of magic milk," she said. "So that Daddy will for sure get this package."

"Magic milk?" Emil snickered.

Hobie felt his face get hot.

"I don't know where she gets these ideas," Mom said. But she helped June bring in a glass for everyone.

"Make a wish with your first swallow," June commanded.

"I wish —" started Uncle Tryg.

"No! No!" June waved her hand, sloshing a little milk. "You can't say your wish out loud."

Emil rolled his eyes. "But we'll all be making the same wish."

"Not out loud," insisted June.

Aunt Ellen raised her eyebrow at Emil.

"Okay," he said. "I'm going to make my wish now." He scrunched his eyes tight. He swallowed loudly. "There," he said.

June watched anxiously as each person drank their magic milk. Then she closed her eyes and drank.

She opened her eyes. "Now Daddy will get his package."

Aunt Ellen wrapped June in a hug. "You better believe it."

CHAPTER SEVENTEEN

Bombs Away

August 30, 1944

June skipped along on the way to her first day of second grade. "I'm going to be the *only* top speller this year," she said. She winked at Hobie. "Magic milk — remember?"

Hobie wasn't too worried about that particular magic spell coming true. June was a whiz when it came to words. He just hoped the other wishing worked. That Dad had gotten his care package. They hadn't heard any more since the postcard.

Hobie dropped June off at her classroom and went on to his new sixth-grade class. He bumped into Catherine in the cloakroom.

"How's that bruise?" she asked.

A ball he'd gone after had taken a bad bounce during their Saturday game. "I'll live," he said, rubbing his shin.

"Too bad Max couldn't play," Catherine said. "That darn paper route."

"Yeah." Hobie got his things and headed into the classroom before she could say anything more about Max. He found a desk with his name on it.

As soon as the final bell rang, Mr. Case began taking roll. "Miss Bunch?"

You could hardly hear her, but Dorine did answer, "Here."

"Mr. Crane?" Mr. Case continued.

"Here," said Preston.

Mr. Case went through the entire classroom, all the way to Mr. Zyskowski, who almost didn't answer because no one ever called him anything but Spud.

Mr. Case and Mrs. Thornton might both be teachers, but that's where the similarity ended. And it wasn't just calling them Miss and Mister. In Mr. Case's class, "young ladies and gentlemen" would be Mastering Mathematics. And Volumizing Vocabulary. And doing Friday Fives.

Hobie liked the sound of Friday Fives because of the extra credit for bringing in some current events newspaper article and talking about it for five minutes. Hobie was pretty sure he was going to need every bit of help he could get in Mr. Case's class.

"Attention, scholars." Mr. Case pulled the cord to roll up the world map at the front of the room. On the chalkboard, underneath the map, was written a poem.

"May I have a volunteer reader?" he asked.

"Poetry?" Mitch muttered. "Spare me."

"Thank you, Mr. —" Mr. Case consulted the seating chart. "Mr. Mitchell."

Mitch looked up to the heavens. "'Autumn,'" he read.

"Stand to recite, please." Mr. Case motioned Mitch up.

Hobie coughed so he wouldn't laugh.

Mitch stood. "'Autumn,'" he repeated in a monotone. "By T. E. Hulme. 'A touch of cold in the Autumn night — I walked abroad, and saw the ruddy moon lean over a hedge.'" He stopped reading. "What's 'ruddy'?"

"Brilliant question, my young scholar." Mr. Case slapped his hands together. "How might you answer it?"

Mitch rubbed his nose. "By asking you?"

"Any other guesses?" Mr. Case scanned the room. "Miss Small?"

"Look it up in the dictionary?" Catherine suggested.

"Smashing. Simply smashing."

A few of the girls giggled. Mr. Case ignored them, focusing again on the seating chart. "Mr. Klein, you are closest to the dictionary. Would you do the honors?"

Max flipped pages and then ran his finger down the page. "Ruddy. The first definition is 'having a healthy reddish color.'" He closed the dictionary.

"So the moon is?" Mr. Case pressed.

"Red!" Dorine blurted out. Twenty-four heads snapped in her direction. Dorine never blurted out. She rarely spoke.

"Nicely done, Miss Bunch." Mr. Case waved at Mitch. "Carry on."

Anyone taking one look at Mitch's face would know he did not want to carry on. But he did.

"'And saw the ruddy moon lean over a hedge. Like a red-faced farmer. I did not stop to speak, but nodded, and round about were the wistful stars with white faces like town children.'"

"Thank you. You may sit down," the teacher said to Mitch. "Any comments about this poem?"

Catherine raised her hand. "It makes a picture in my mind. Like a photograph."

"Good. Anyone else?"

"It's short?" Marty offered hesitantly.

"That it is." Mr. Case swung his arms as if directing an orchestra. "Which will make it all the easier for you scholars to memorize." He smiled from ear to ear. "By Monday."

The mutterings were drowned out by the lunch bell.

"Eat, drink, and be merry," Mr. Case said, waving them off to the cafeteria.

"This year's certainly going to be interesting," Catherine said as she pulled her lunch pail out of the cubby.

"You said it," Hobie agreed. While he waited his turn for hot lunch, that line about the stars with faces like town children came back to him. It made sense even if he didn't know exactly what it meant.

The cafeteria ladies filled his plate, and he handed over his coins at the cash register, noting that Marty had plunked down next to Max. Hobie took a free seat at the other end of the boys' table. Unfortunately, Mitch took the seat directly across.

"So, Hobie." Mitch took a loud slurp of milk. "My mom told me about your old man. Prisoner of war camp. That's tough."

Hobie felt like he was walking into some kind of trap. Mitch Mitchell being nice?

"I have a question." Mitch's tone reminded Hobie of the vacuum cleaner salesman who'd stopped at their house a while back.

Hobie squeezed some ketchup on his meat loaf. "Okay."

"Well, say you were in the Army Air Force, and some lousy Nazis captured you and stuck you in some camp, wouldn't you try to escape?" he asked. "My brother's a regular old GI, and that's what he says he'd do."

Mitch leaned across the table, so close Hobie could smell his milky breath. "That's what any true blue American would do." He emphasized the word "American." "Don't you think?"

Hobie stared at him. Mitch was a fathead, but whoever thought he'd stoop *this* low?

"*You're* un-American," Preston said. "Talking about a soldier that way."

"Yeah, take it back," added a fifth-grade kid. A big fifth-grade kid.

The other boys stopped chewing and swallowing and burping to listen. To see what Hobie would do.

"At least my dad enlisted," Hobie said. "That's more than your dad did." He pushed back on the stool and picked up his tray.

The stool Max had been sitting in was empty. Hobie took it.

"Are you okay?" Marty asked. He moved his tray to make room for Hobie's.

Hobie told him what Mitch had said.

"What a creep," Marty said.

"You can say that again." Hobie pushed his lunch around on his plate until the recess bell rang. Then he went outside and played tetherball. Each time the ball swung around, he imagined he was punching Mitch, not the ball. He won every single game.

Walking home from school, Hobie was still as hot as he'd been at lunchtime. The only thing that simmered him down was the hope that one of these days, Mitch would get what he deserved.

June skipped along beside him, lips purple from feasting on the ripe blackberries brushing up against the sidewalk.

"Do you want to pick some berries later?" she asked. "Mom could make a pie."

"I've got homework."

"Then Kitty and I will pick." June set her hands on her hips. "And you won't get any pie."

"See if I care." Hobie stomped up the front steps, stopping to get the mail. He flipped through the envelopes. There was one addressed to him. From Pearl Harbor. He didn't know anybody there. And he didn't recognize the handwriting.

He dropped his books on the porch, perched on the railing, and opened it.

Dear Hobie,

I am Merna Watts, a nurse at the naval base here on Pearl Harbor. Pfc. Corff is one of my patients. He has asked me to take dictation for him. He told me all about you. You sound like a fine young man. I don't know what he would have done without Duke. Now, these words from my impatient patient:

Hey, there, pardner,

Looks like me and Duke have earned ourselves a vacation from the war. I wanted you to hear the skinny from me, not from anyone else. I owe you that.

Hobie's heart tightened as he read those words, not sure he could read further. But he had to. Had to find out.

You may have heard or read about the battle on Guam. It was a scrap, let me tell you. And we were holding our own. Until July 27 or 28. I kind of lost track of time.

There were four of us scouting with a patrol — my buddy Ski and his dog, Missy, and me and Duke. It was dark and we were deep in the jungle. Bugs and vines and all kinds of things to trip you up.

The enemy had been on the island a lot longer than we had. Knew every hiding place around. I swear, they can hide in plain sight. After an hour or so, Missy picked up a scent and we got ourselves into a little pickle. Came out with three prisoners and no injuries. We were feeling pretty smart about the entire situation.

Then the lieutenant gave the order to march on, but Duke had other ideas. I hollered for everyone to hit the deck. That darned dog took the bullets meant for me. I tried to drag him to a foxhole and found myself with a few new holes, too.

When the coast was clear, the medics were Johnny-on-the-spot. Ski tried to get Duke back to camp, to the vet. But no go. Duke was on me like a tick. The medics wanted to leave him behind, but me and Ski and Missy helped change their minds.

Don't worry — Duke's going to be fine. He gets treated like a general here. And, because of him, I get treated okay, too.

Semper Fi,

Marv

Hobie should have seen it coming. Every headline blared some battle news from the Pacific. And the movies and newsreels always showed the Marines with the worst jobs: first in, cleanup, that sort of thing. But he never thought anything like this could happen. Even though Marv tried to put a good spin on it, things were bad. Hobie was sure of it.

"Tell Mom I'll be back later," he hollered to June. He grabbed his bike and pedaled as fast as he could. He didn't have a plan. He simply had to ride.

Trees and houses and people swirled. It was like that storm scene in the *Wizard of Oz* movie. Everything gray and spinning so fast, Hobie couldn't make anything out. He kept riding, turning up one street, turning down the next.

Without realizing it, he'd found his way to Fishermen's Terminal. He slowed down, easing the bike's tires over the uneven wooden dock planks until he was at the slip where the *Lily Bess* was moored. Uncle Tryg was topside, sanding a rail.

"Well, ahoy, there," he called out to Hobie. "Come aboard."

Hobie set his bike down and clambered over the gangplank.

"Need some help?" Hobie asked.

"On this bucket of bolts?" Uncle Tryg's laugh was like an arm around his shoulder, making Hobie feel that everything was going to be okay. "Always."

He tossed Hobie a rag to wipe down the rail, then started in on a patch of blistered paint.

Hobie followed behind his uncle, rubbing and rubbing until there wasn't a single grain of sawdust. The late afternoon sun pounded down. Beads of sweat scrabbled down his back like a thousand spiders. He thought of the bugs in that jungle where Duke and Marv had been, and shivered.

"Someone step on your grave?" Unce Tryg must have noticed the shiver.

Hobie wiped the rail even harder. He hadn't planned to say anything, but the news was like a fish trying to wiggle out of a net. "I got a letter. About Duke."

Uncle Tryg stopped sanding. "Everything okay?"

Suddenly Hobie's legs wouldn't hold him up anymore. He slid to the deck. "They were almost killed."

Uncle Tryg eased to sit on a nearby bucket. "You want to tell me about it?"

Hobie did. He told his uncle everything in Marv's letter. And he didn't stop there. He told him about trying to get Duke back. About messing up with

Max. About Mitch. Every part of his body was shaking by the time he was done. Even his teeth were chattering.

Uncle Tryg didn't say anything when Hobie finished. He probably was ashamed of him. Hobie leaned his forehead on his knees.

"All right." The bucket scraped against the deck as Uncle Tryg stood up. "Time to stain." He pried open a can of stain and tossed Hobie another rag. They wiped it back and forth, back and forth across the sanded wood. Hobie's nails turned as dark as the dirt in their Victory garden.

"Do you know the story of my arm?"

They'd been quiet for so long, Hobie jumped at Uncle Tryg's voice.

"It got caught in a winch," Hobie said.

Uncle Tryg wiped at the sweat on his forehead with the back of his hand. "That's part of it." The rubbing left a spot of stain. "Our father was a tough old bird. Strict. Oh, man, you did not want to sail against his rules." Uncle Tryg whistled. "He probably turns over in his grave watching down on my boys."

Hobie dipped his rag in the stain can again.

Uncle Tryg sighed. "Young men and their fathers. There's bound to be some butting of heads. Especially on a boat."

Hobie couldn't imagine butting heads with Dad. As if reading his mind, Uncle Tryg said, "You wait. It happens. Part of life."

"So you and Grandfather didn't get along?" Hobie asked.

"Oh, we got along fine. As long as I did everything he said." Uncle Tryg looked out over the bow of the *Lily Bess*, out beyond the breakwater. Hobie wondered what he was looking at.

"So one night, I'm sixteen years old and tired of my father's dos and don'ts. I go out with my friends. Watch a ball game. Drink some beers." He leaned into Hobie. "Don't tell Aunt Ellen I told you that part. My boys don't even know."

Hobie crossed his hand over his heart.

"I wasn't feeling so hot the next morning. But if you're a Hanson, you're on the boat, hungover or not. I was green as bilgewater, and not thinking straight. I figured I'd rest a bit when I got aboard. So what if the ropes didn't get rolled up just so." Uncle Tryg held up his arm. "I learned it the hard way, Hobie." Uncle Tryg started in on the rail again.

Hobie waited.

Nothing more came.

"What did you learn the hard way?" he asked.

Uncle Tryg rubbed the rag back and forth, back and forth, coating the rail with stain. He didn't look up. "*My* lesson," he said. "Each man to his own."

Hobie had never had a conversation like this with Uncle Tryg before. Never had a conversation like this with any adult before. Something shifted a bit inside him. He felt like somehow he'd just taken a first big step away from being a boy toward being a man.

Uncle Tryg rubbed the rail a few more times.

"I'm ready to call it a day," he said. "Let's clean up. I'll give you a ride home."

Every tool had to be spotless before it could be stowed away. Finally, Uncle Tryg locked up the cabin and they climbed back across the gangplank. Hobie picked up his bike and pushed it along the dock.

"Hold up a second." Uncle Tryg fished some coins from his pocket and bought two grape Nehis from the machine at the net shed. Hobie nearly downed his in one guzzle, he was that thirsty.

At the car, Uncle Tryg unlocked the trunk and Hobie lifted his bike in. "You did good work today," Uncle Tryg told him as they both closed their car doors.

"Thanks." Hobie rolled down the window to let out a little of the smell of sweat and oily stain.

There wasn't any conversation the rest of the way home. So Hobie had time to think about what his uncle had said. What had Uncle Tryg learned? Hobie wasn't sure.

Hobie had never done anything quite like what Uncle Tryg described. But he sure had gotten some ropes tangled lately. Especially with Max. And trying to get Duke back? What would have happened to Marv and Missy and those other guys if he had?

He leaned back against the seat. Enlisting Duke had been the hardest thing he'd ever done. Ever. It must be sort of like Uncle Tryg, living with a bad arm because of one dumb decision. And Dad. Hobie had always thought he was brave because he was fighting in the war. But maybe the bravest thing he did was leave behind the people that he loved for something he believed in.

So maybe Hobie wasn't like his Grandfather Hanson, steaming full speed ahead through life, like a giant destroyer. He was more like a little skiff, bumping along against the waves. The thing is, eventually, both boats reach the shore.

Maybe there were different kinds of bravery. Grandfather Hanson's kind. Dad and Uncle Tryg's kind.

And Hobie's kind. The kind that doesn't roar.

Hobie was startled when Uncle Tryg said, "Here you are." They were at Hobie's house already.

Uncle Tryg tapped Hobie on the arm. "Next season, we'll all be on the boat," he said. "You, your dad, and me and my boys. You wait and see."

Hobie pulled his bike out of the trunk and waved good-bye. When Uncle Tryg said a thing, a guy could count on it.

"Next season." He liked the sound of those words.

Dinner smells beckoned to him from the house. He hurried inside.

Uncle Tryg said it would be good next season.

But Hobie had a feeling he could make some things good right now.

CHAPTER EIGHTEEN

Gum and Gumption

August 31, 1944

Hobie hurried to the paper shack right after school. He didn't have to wait long before a big truck pulled up. Shortly after that, the first of the newspaper carriers arrived, getting their allotted papers from the driver and taking them over to the shack to fold them.

When Max showed up, Pepper ran straight over to Hobie, licking his hands.

"What are you doing here?" Max set his bike on the ground. "Did you get a route?"

"Nope." Hobie rubbed the top of Pepper's head.

"Then what are you doing?" Max walked over to the truck and grabbed a bundle of papers.

Hobie grabbed a bundle, too, shifting it to his shoulder. It was heavy. "Where do these go?"

Max fumbled with the load he'd grabbed. "I don't need your help," he said.

"This is heavy," Hobie said. "I'd like to put it down."

Max stared at Hobie. Hobie stared back.

"Okay. Over there." Max pointed to a spot next to the shed. "Only the older guys work inside," he explained. "Unless it's raining."

Hobie put the papers where Max showed him and grabbed another load. After several trips, Max said, "That's all I get." He plunked to the ground, cut the twine around a bundle of papers with his pocketknife, and began folding. Pepper curled up behind him, like a furry backrest.

"That looks kind of tricky." Hobie sat down, too. "Want to show me how?"

"What are you doing?" Max asked.

Hobie picked up a newspaper and started to fold it. "I figured I'd help my friend with his paper route." He tried to make the same folds Max was making. "So he could get done in time to listen to *Hop Harrigan* with me." He looked over at Max.

Max looked right back. Then he grabbed the newspaper from Hobie. "It's going to fall apart if you fold it like that. Here." He showed Hobie what to do.

It took him several tries, but Hobie got the hang of it. When all the papers were folded, Hobie ran over to his bike to grab the canvas shopping bag he'd brought. "I figured we could each carry half."

Max pulled two pieces of Black Jack gum from his pocket. He handed one to Hobie, and put the other in his mouth. Then he tugged his carrier bag over his shoulder. "How's your throwing arm?" he said.

"Pretty good, after playing baseball most of the summer." Hobie unwrapped his piece of gum and popped it in his mouth. Working on the boat had sprouted him some muscles, too. "Lead the way." He hopped on his bike.

Pepper danced all around when she saw Max get on his bike. "Crazy dog," Max said.

"Duke's like that, too." Hobie followed Max down the sidewalk.

When they got to the first street on Max's route, Max pointed out which houses needed papers. Hobie tossed them on one side of the street and Max on the other. As they rode, Hobie noticed how many of the houses had blue star flags in the window, like the one they had at home. He noticed some with gold stars, too. He hoped no one he knew ever had to change their blue star to gold.

About the fifth house, Hobie missed the porch. He slowed his bike to get off and grab the paper.

"Pepper!" Max called. "Paper!" He pointed toward Hobie.

Like a black-and-white blur, Pepper flashed past Hobie, picked up the wayward paper, and ran it to the porch.

Hobie shook his head. "Maybe you don't need my help after all, with Pepper around."

"Sometimes I miss on purpose," Max said. "Just to keep her on her toes."

They finished that block and turned up the next.

Mitch Mitchell's street. And there was Mitch Mitchell's house.

Hobie glanced over at Max. "You deliver here?"

Max reached into his bag. "His mom's a good tipper."

Hobie felt every muscle in his body tense up. But the house looked empty. The shades were drawn on the front windows. No car in the driveway.

Nobody home.

"Hey, look." Hobie pointed to a pair of sneakers on the front porch. Mitch Mitchell–sized sneakers.

"So?" Max grabbed another paper out of his bag and got ready to throw.

Hobie braked to a halt. He held out his hand. "Give me your gum."

"What?" Max made a face. "Disgusting."

Hobie spit his own wad of gum into his hand. "Yeah. Isn't it?"

Max laughed. "I get it." He spit out his gum and tossed it to Hobie.

Hobie jumped off his bike and tiptoed up the Mitchells' front steps. With a quick glance over his shoulder, he picked up one of the sneakers. He pushed his piece of gum into the very tip of the toe. He did the same with the other sneaker and Max's gum. Wiping his hands on his dungarees, he bounded down the steps.

"'Who knows what evil lurks in the hearts of men?'" Max said the words just like a radio announcer.

"'The Shadow knows,'" Hobie answered, jumping back on his bike. "And us!"

They rode away, gumless and hysterical.

Pepper rescued a couple more papers while they finished the route. When the last paper was tossed, the boys turned and headed for Hobie's house, Pepper hot on their tails.

The boys dropped their bikes on the front lawn and tore up the stairs. Hobie cranked on the radio. The announcer's voice filled the kitchen with *"Hop Harrigan, Ace of the Airways!"*

"We made it!" Max slid into a chair.

Hobie turned up the volume and then sat down, too.

After sniffing around for crumbs, without success, Pepper curled up under the table.

June and Kitty crawled under the table, too. "You get to listen with your friend," she said. "So we're going to listen with ours."

Hobie chuckled about what he and Max had done. Scooter would be proud.

"Want a piece of gum?" he asked.

Max sputtered.

"I want some." June poked her head out from under the table.

That got the boys laughing so hard they missed Hop Harrigan's opening lines.

CHAPTER NINETEEN

A Gold Star in the Window

October 19, 1944

Hobie snagged the mail from the box. "Dad!" he hollered, waving the postcard as he ran inside.

Mom grabbed it from him and began to read.

I am the envy of all in my barracks. Simply holding the care package was like a furlough from this place. I have shared everything, as we do here. Junebug, your artwork is treated like an old master. And, Hobie, the joke book has already been passed around so much the cover is falling off. My love to you all. Aim, fly, fight.

June jumped up and down. "The magic milk worked," she said. "It worked!"

Mom scooped her in a big hug. "It certainly did." She winked at Hobie.

After dinner, Hobie practiced reciting the week's poem to Mom and June. And Kitty.

"This poem is called, 'An Autumn Greeting,' and it's by Anonymous."

June clapped.

Hobie cleared his throat.

> *"Come," said the Wind to the Leaves one day.*
> *"Come over the meadow and we will play.*
> *"Put on your dresses of red and gold*
> *"For summer is gone and the days grow cold."*

Mom applauded. "Very dramatic," she said.

"That one was kind of short," said June. "Thank goodness."

"June!" Mom play-spanked her.

"Wait till you hear the one for next week," Hobie said. "It goes on forever."

"Oh no." June put her hands over her ears.

"You two!" Mom began to clear the table. "A little culture will do you both good."

Hobie looked at June and crossed his eyes. She pressed Kitty to her mouth to smother her giggle.

At school the next day, Hobie passed Mrs. Thornton in the hallway as he was returning from the boys' room.

"Hobie!" She greeted him warmly. "You haven't forgotten me, now that you're a big sixth grader, have you?"

He felt his face get hot. "No."

"What good luck that I've run into you." Mrs. Thornton tugged on the locket at her neck. "I've got a bookcase that needs moving. Would you be able to help at lunchtime?"

"Sure." Hobie waved. "See you then."

Later, as his class lined up for lunch, Hobie saw the principal, Miss Maynard, motion Mrs. Thornton into the hall, leaning into her with a whisper. Mrs. Thornton looked up, startled, then hurried toward the office. As Miss Maynard stepped into the fifth-grade classroom, Hobie heard her say, "Class, I need your attention."

Catherine Small carried the news to the sixth-grade lunch table. Her eyes and nose were red and her words came out in jagged chunks. "He was killed in action," she said. "Mr. Thornton. In Italy."

Other girls' sobs joined Catherine's. None of the

boys could cry, of course. Not at school. But there was plenty of throat clearing.

Their beautiful movie-star teacher and her movie-star husband. It couldn't be true. Couldn't be possible.

When they returned to the classroom, Mr. Case confirmed Catherine's report. "I know you children are very fond of Mrs. Thornton," he said, clearing his own throat several times. "I'm sure you and your families will keep her in your prayers." He slumped at his desk.

After a few moments, Dorine raised her hand. "Mr. Case? Shall we work on our essays?"

He looked startled, as if surprised to find himself in the teacher's chair. "Yes. Yes. Good idea." He picked up a pen and began to scribble in the notebook he kept on his desk.

Somehow the sixth graders made it through the rest of the day. The classroom had been quiet. Too quiet. That all changed the minute the last bell rang, in the cloakroom.

Mitch flew at Max, tackling him to the ground. "You dirty Kraut!" Mitch screamed. "It's all your fault."

"Knock it off." Marty struggled to pull Mitch and Max apart. "Max didn't do anything."

A tear ran down Mitch's face. Hobie saw it before he swiped it away.

"Dirty Germans," Mitch yelled. "And he's one of them." He drew his fist back. Hobie wasn't sure what would be left of Max once Mitch got started. He didn't know what to do.

"Go ahead," Max said, getting to his feet. He could have been a cucumber, he was that cool. Hobie had no idea how he could be. *He* was trembling.

"Hit me." Max lifted up his chin.

Mitch stopped.

"Max!" Hobie couldn't help himself. "What are you doing?"

Catherine rushed up. "What's going on?"

Max locked gazes with Mitch. It was a game of chicken. Who would turn away first?

"I feel as bad as you do," Max continued, staring right at Mitch. "About Mrs. Thornton."

Hobie moved next to his friend, his eyes locked in on Mitch's, just like Duke that time. "If it makes you feel better, you can hit me, too." Hobie's legs were Jell-O, but he didn't move from Max's side.

A few of the other sixth graders crowded closer. Stood alongside Hobie and Max.

Marty. Preston. Catherine. Dorine.

Mitch's fists dropped. "You guys are nutso," he said. He brushed off his clothes and marched away.

"You guys *are* nutso," Catherie said, punching both Hobie and Max on the arm. But there was pride in her voice. "He could have killed you."

Hobie rubbed his arm. "Yeah. Nutso." He was suddenly very sad. He hadn't helped Mrs. Thornton with that bookcase.

"I would've punched the first German I saw, too," Catherine admitted. "If I'd seen one." She nudged Max with her shoulder.

Max reached into his pocket and pulled out a pack of Black Jack gum. He gave Hobie and Catherine each a piece.

And then he put the pack back in his pocket.

CHAPTER TWENTY

Santa Comes Early

December 18, 1944

"You'll wear out that window," Mom teased as Hobie made his tenth trip through the front room.

"You don't think he got lost?" Hobie asked. Marv wasn't from Seattle. He might have a hard time finding his way around.

"He'll be here soon." Mom straightened the collar on Hobie's shirt.

Hobie ducked away before she could fuss with his hair. He had waited so long for this day to come. And now, finally, finally Duke would be home. Away from the jungle snakes and bugs and Japanese soldiers.

"Will Duke remember us?" June asked.

"He'll remember." Hobie picked up a comic book, scanning the same page a dozen times. He knew Duke would remember them. What he hoped was that Marv wouldn't remember the letters. The ones asking for Duke back. That thought tugged Hobie's spirits down as if it was an anchor as heavy as the one on the *Lily Bess*.

Just when he thought he might turn inside out with the misery of waiting, an old jalopy rattled to a stop in front of their house.

"They're here!" Hobie tore out the door and down the steps, skidding to a stop at the curb. The driver's door popped open, and Hobie stepped back. Even though he and Marv had been writing back and forth all this time, they were strangers.

"Hobie!" Marv slid out from under the steering wheel and out of the car. "Man, it's good to meet you!" When he smiled, the scar across his cheek and eyebrow puckered. But that smile made Hobie feel at ease. Marv was old — twenty-two — but he looked younger than Hobie thought he would.

Marv limped a few steps to open the back door. "Here's the guy you've really been waiting for."

Duke shook himself in the backseat, and Hobie's breath caught in his chest. Duke was thinner than when he'd left. More muscular, too. His ears twitched when he saw Hobie and his tail tick-tocked, but he didn't move.

"It's okay, Duke," Marv said. "Go."

At Marv's words, Duke bounded forward, waggling his long body and licking Hobie all at the same time. A few tears snuck out. Duke licked them away.

"He sure is glad to be home," Marv said.

"Yeah." Hobie choked the word out.

Mom stood on the porch, wiping her eyes with her apron. "Come on in, you boys. I've got lunch all ready."

Marv took the steps one at a time. *Step-thump. Step-thump.* A ring of white formed around his mouth as he made his way up. But he didn't say a word. Hobie guessed that his leg must hurt. A lot.

Mom introduced herself and June, and they all went into the kitchen. Hobie had put Duke's blanket right by the stove, in his favorite place. But Duke stayed glued to Marv's side.

"Hey, boy, no." Marv gestured with his hand. "You can't be at the table." He caught sight of the blanket and told Duke, "Down." Duke sighed, but padded to the corner and, after turning around three times, flopped on the blanket.

"Ever since I took that bullet, he doesn't want to leave me alone," said Marv. "The darn dog would follow me into the latrine, if I let him."

"He's very loyal," Mom said, setting a big platter of sandwiches on the table.

"And that's only the half of it." Marv took one sandwich.

"Oh, take another," Mom said. "You look like you could use some fattening up."

"Well, K-rations will do that to you." Marv opened his napkin. "And various jungle ailments."

Hobie took a sandwich when the platter was passed his way. But he wasn't all that hungry.

"Will your leg get better?" Hobie asked, peeling off the crust.

"Hobie!" Mom scolded. She made a face that said, "That's not a question to ask."

"It's okay, ma'am." Marv set down his sandwich. "Good buddies can ask each other stuff. And me and Hobie are good buddies." He leaned forward. "Let me put it this way. The leg won't get better, but I'll get better at using it." Marv glanced over at Duke. "If it weren't for that guy over there, I wouldn't be here at all."

They all sat quietly for a few minutes. Hobie thought about what Marv had written him from the hospital. What Duke had done to protect Marv.

And what he'd done afterward, too, staying with him, bullets flying, until the medics came, despite his own wounds. Tears burned at the back of his eyes. He felt worse than ever about writing those letters.

Mom poured Marv a cup of coffee. "Dogs truly are a man's best friend."

"You got that right." Marv took a sip. "Duke and his buddies sure made Uncle Sam proud."

Hearing his name, Duke stirred. Hobie watched him watching Marv. Duke's brown eyes tracked every move Marv made.

"That was delicious, ma'am," Marv said. "Thank you so much." He turned to Hobie. "Hey, buddy. Wanna play some catch?"

They went outside, Duke on their heels, and tossed the ball back and forth. "You've got a good arm there," Marv told Hobie. He showed him how to get under a pop fly and how to scoop up a grounder. His bum leg didn't seem to hurt his catching skills.

Mom called them in for some dessert. Hobie hesitated.

"Can I ask you another question?" he said.

"Shoot." Marv rolled the ball between his hands.

Mom had warned Hobie not to press Marv about what happened the day he got hurt. But there was something he wanted to know. "You said the lieutenant gave the all clear. What made you know that it wasn't all clear?"

"I didn't know," Marv said. He tipped his head toward Duke, on the ground next to them. "But *he* did. It was just like you told me. His ears perked up and I knew there was trouble." Marv leaned over and scratched Duke's head. "This guy saved a lot of lives that day." He sat up and looked at Hobie. "*You* saved a lot of lives that day."

Goose bumps broke out on Hobie's arms. What if he hadn't told Marv about Duke's warning signal? Who knows what would have happened to that patrol. To Marv. To Duke. Thinking about it made Hobie's hands shake. He tucked them behind his back so Marv wouldn't see. Who would have thought that doing the right thing could be something as small as writing a letter?

Writing a letter. Hobie swallowed. Hard. "I wish I hadn't written those letters," he said. He couldn't even look at Marv.

Marv nodded. "I know." He winked. "The bit about your sister was good," he said.

Hobie's face burned.

"Hey." Marv tapped him on the arm. "Forget about it. If you hadn't wanted Duke back, I would've thought there was something wrong with you. In the end, you did the right thing, Hobie. That's what counts. Savvy?" He bent down to catch Hobie's eye. "We're square," he said. "More than square."

Hobie met Marv's eyes. He could tell he meant what he was saying. That anchor unhooked itself from Hobie's heart.

Duke got up and stretched, head down, hind end in the air.

"Now, I've got a question for you," said Marv. "Why do dogs run in circles?"

Hobie grinned. "Because it's hard to run in squares."

Marv chuckled. "Well, I tried."

"Are you boys coming in?" Mom called again.

"For dessert? Yes, ma'am!" Marv made his way slowly and stiffly up the back steps, to the kitchen, where Mom had huge slices of cake waiting for them.

After the last crumb was devoured, Marv pushed himself off the chair, struggling to stand. "Well, pardner. This was a real nice day. I'm so glad I got to meet you and your family."

Marv thanked Mom again for lunch. "I've got to take off for now — some things to do in town. But I was wondering if I could come back tomorrow morning, before I go home to Ohio." He rubbed his hand over his mouth. "To say good-bye to old Duke here."

"Of course!" Mom said. She'd wrapped up some sandwiches and cake and pressed those on Marv.

But Marv was looking at Hobie. Waiting for *him* to answer.

"Sure," he said, clearing his throat. "Of course."

"Hey, pard, there's something I completely forgot to tell you." Marv shifted to stand on his good leg. "About Duke."

Hobie caught his breath. Was Marv going to ask to keep him? And if he did, what would Hobie do?

"And Missy," Marv continued. "Even though Uncle Sam said 'verboten' to fraternization, those two" — he turned his head away from Mom and June and coughed — "met up. We think it was sometime in Pearl Harbor." Marv scratched his head. "The upshot is six puppies. Spitting image of their dad."

"Puppies?" June said.

"Yep." Marv winked. "And there is a little girl named Duchess that will be going home with this soldier" — he jabbed his thumb at himself — "as soon as she gets out of quarantine."

"Hobie, are you crying?" June asked.

"No!" Hobie said. "I've got something in my eye."

Marv tapped Hobie on the shoulder, then snapped off a salute. "Semper Fi, buddy." He reached over and stroked Duke's head. "Semper Fi."

The Marine Corps' motto. Semper Fidelis. *Always faithful.* Semper Fi. "Semper Fido!" Hobie blurted out.

Marv laughed. "You said it." He limped to the door and down the stairs.

Duke followed.

Marv pulled open the car door. Duke nosed his way inside. Like he wanted to go, too.

Hobie froze. Should he call him? Let him come on his own? What if he called and Duke didn't come? He felt like he was on the *Lily Bess,* tossed up and down by stormy seas.

Marv gave Duke a pat. "You take care, buddy."

Duke licked Marv's face. He hopped out of the car and ran to Hobie.

Marv closed the door, his arm out the open window. "See you tomorrow!"

Duke barked. Then he dove under the rhody bush, digging up a ball he'd left there who knows when. He trotted up to Hobie, nudging the dirty ball into his hand.

Hobie's heart felt like it might float right out of his chest, he was that happy. He ruffled Duke's fur. Then he took the ball and threw it as far as he could.

And before it hit the ground, Duke snagged it. He trotted back, ball in mouth, ready for more.

Just like Hobie.

CHAPTER TWENTY-ONE

Victory in Europe!

May 8, 1945

On Victory in Europe — V-E — Day, Hobie, Mom, and June got up at six in the morning to listen to President Truman's speech. Uncle Tryg's family came over to listen with them.

The president's voice was soft and sad as he spoke. "I only wish that Franklin D. Roosevelt had lived to witness this day," he said, right off the bat.

That made Mom sniffle and reach for her hanky.

Uncle Tryg put his hand over his heart. "That was a good man," he said. "A good man."

Hobie got the chills when President Truman talked about the flags of freedom flying all over Europe. Maybe they were flying over Dad, too, in Stalag Luft 1.

There was a knock at the door. Hobie opened it to find Max and Pepper.

"Come on!" Max shouted, his arms full of old newspapers.

Emil, Erik, and Duke ran out the door behind Hobie.

They shredded the papers into tiny bits. Then they ran up and down the street, tossing the scraps and hollering. Duke and Pepper followed along, howling and barking, howling and barking. Somewhere along the way, the boys found some dented pots and pans that they beat with abandon.

"Hear, hear!" Mr. Gilbert cheered them on from his porch.

"Well done," shouted Mrs. Lee, her hair still in pin curls.

"Hooray!" called Catherine Small. She came running out of her house to join them. Hobie handed her a fistful of confetti.

When they ran out of energy and paper, they ended up back at Hobie's, where Mom was cutting into her freshly baked "Victory coffee cake." "Who wants the first slice?" she asked.

At that moment, the doorbell rang. Uncle Tryg set down his coffee cup and went to answer it. He came back holding a telegram. Mom's face whitened. She read it and then burst into tears.

Hobie grabbed Duke's collar.

Mom pressed her hand to her mouth, handing the telegram over to Uncle Tryg. He read it, then grabbed Mom and spun her around. *"Takk Gud!"* he shouted. "Thank God!"

"The camp was liberated! May first!" Mom laughed and cried all at the same time. "Dad's free!"

"Free!" cried June, swinging Kitty above her head. "I'm going to give him my spelling ribbons!"

Uncle Tryg held out the telegram for Hobie to read.

Dad. A prisoner of war no more. "When's he coming home?" Hobie asked, trying to take it all in.

Mom put her hand to her cheek. "A month. Maybe two?" She mussed up Hobie's hair. "We are going to have quite the party," she said.

"I'll bring cookies," said Catherine.

"And I'll bring Pepper!" cried Max.

"And I'll bring the best thing of all," said Hobie. "My dad."

CHAPTER TWENTY-TWO

Hobie Hanson Calling the Control Tower

June 30, 1945

Hobie stepped into the kitchen, sniffing. Mom had two pies cooling and a cake in the oven for Dad's homecoming party. She brushed her hands on her apron. "I'm nearly out of sugar. Can you run to Lee's for me?" Of course, she thought of a few other items to add to the grocery list. Hobie would have gladly carted home an elephant, he was that happy.

He whistled for Duke and they headed out. Duke loped alongside the bike, grinning. Marv said Duchess grinned like that, too. Especially when she chased squirrels. *Like father, like daughter,* Marv had written in his last letter, postmarked from Botkins, Ohio, his hometown.

Hobie turned the last corner toward Lee's. Across the street he saw the little girl with her dog, Suzy.

"Hey!" Hobie called out, waving.

"Hey!" The girl called back. "Look at this!" She stopped right on the sidewalk and told Suzy to sit, down, stay.

Suzy performed like a champ.

"Hot dog!" Hobie cheered.

"Thank you!" The girl waved as Hobie rode off.

When he got to Lee's, Hobie parked his bike out front like always, but now Duke followed him up the steps. Mrs. Lee had changed her rules. "War veterans welcome," she'd proclaimed. "Especially the four-legged kind."

The bell over the door tinkled as they stepped inside. Mrs. Lee put her feather duster down and pulled a Milk-Bone from her apron pocket. Duke crunched it happily.

"*I've* got a joke for *you* today," she told Hobie, scratching behind Duke's ears. "What do dogs have that no other animals have?"

That was an old one, but Hobie pretended he'd never heard it. "I give," he said.

"Puppies!" Mrs. Lee tapped the countertop. "Get it?"

Hobie got it.

Mrs. Lee gathered up the sugar and other items

on Mom's list while Hobie counted out the ration stamps, handing them over with the money.

"Are you coming to Dad's welcome home party?" he asked. He never got tired of saying those delicious words together: "Dad" and "home."

"Wouldn't miss it. I'm bringing my famous sauerkraut cake," she said. "It's always a hit."

"That'd be . . . swell." Sauerkraut cake didn't sound like a hit. But Hobie didn't want to hurt Mrs. Lee's feelings. "See you in the funny papers!"

He adjusted the canvas bag on his back, threw his leg over his bike, and started off. As they passed the playfield, Duke drew a bead on a squirrel. Hobie eased to a stop and watched the chase. The squirrels always won, but that would never discourage Duke.

The smell of cigarette smoke tweaked Hobie's nose. He glanced around. There, by the playfield backstop, stood Mitch Mitchell with a bunch of guys. Older guys. Hobie watched them for a second. They were passing around a pack of cigarettes. Probably kiped from someone's dad. Mitch was busy showing off, blowing smoke rings.

Hobie began riding again, knowing Duke would

soon find his way home. A block away, Hobie ran into one of the ladies in Mom's Red Cross group.

"Hobie," she called.

He slowed his bike.

"Such good news about your father," she said. "We can't wait until our Mike gets home. Whenever that will be." She sighed. "You give my best to your mother, will you?"

Hobie nodded. Then remembered his manners. "Thank you, Mrs. Mitchell."

"Time to be on my way," she said. "I'm headed to Lee's to pick up some pudding mix. Mitch does love his tapioca!"

Hobie told Mrs. Mitchell good-bye and placed his feet on the bike pedals. "And say hello to Mitch for me," he added.

"I'll do that, next time I see him," she said.

According to Hobie's calculations, that would be in about one minute.

Hobie whistled. Duke came running. Running to Hobie.

"Want to race, boy?" Hobie cranked on the pedals, ready to ride, ready to fly.

"This time," he said, "I just might beat you."

AUTHOR'S NOTE

Not too long ago, I visited a school where a boy asked me if all my stories were about war. The answer is that none of my stories are *about* war. I like to write about *people* who are dealing with tough times. Like wars.

When I started this book, my plan was to write about a boy whose father was an American prisoner of war in Germany. The goal was to honor my husband's uncle, Palmer Bruland, who flew B-24s in World War II. Palmer had wanted to get home to his wife and family, so he signed on for an extra mission, the Kassel Mission, in a plane he'd never flown (*The Texas Rose*) with a crew he'd never met. The Kassel Mission was a disaster for the Allies; barely half the men survived. Palmer's plane was shot down; he was captured and sent to Stalag Luft 1 in Barth, Germany. By the time that camp was liberated on May 1, 1945, it housed 8,939 officers from America, Britain, Canada, and New Zealand, who were all many, many pounds thinner after a long winter without sufficient food.

I read dozens and dozens of POW memoirs, and was powerfully moved by those stories, but I kept reading, intent on discovering what wartime life was like for *kids*.

In one of the books I read, *"Daddy's Gone to War": The Second World War in the Lives of America's Children*, by William M. Tuttle, Jr., I came across an absolutely astonishing description of how kids helped with the war effort: "In addition to scrap collecting, school age children sent books, magazines, and crossword puzzles to patients in veterans' hospitals. Children also . . . ***volunteered their pet dogs for service***" (p. 124; emphasis added).

I had to read those sentences several times. I couldn't believe it. Children volunteered their pets? In all of my reading about World War II, I had never before encountered this fact.

But, indeed, it was true. Through an organization called Dogs for Defense, thousands of family pets were "enlisted" in Uncle Sam's Army. A good number stayed stateside and worked as guard dogs, patrolling plants that made airplanes and other important matériel for the war. But many dogs saw action, serving as messengers, sentries, on patrols, and as bomb and mine sniffers.

You should know that I am owned by an adorable dog named Winston (a.k.a. Winston the Wonder Dog). I cannot imagine sending him off to war. It would break my heart! But that's because I'm living now. Had I lived back during WWII, I might have felt quite differently. Then, people at home were bombarded with constant pleas to pitch in and do their bit. Newspaper and magazine ads and articles, radio shows, comic books, and movies — even cartoon characters! — urged Americans to do all they could for the war effort. I began to understand how a boy like Hobie would feel pressured to send away his beloved dog, especially if he believed it might help the war end sooner.

Some of you will wonder if this story is true. Let me answer this way: There was a program called Dogs for Defense (Seattle twins Spike and Mike Jankelson did give up their Collie, Laddie) as well as a place called Stalag Luft 1, and a radio show about Hop Harrigan (Hobie would have listened to it every afternoon, on station KJR).

Lee's Grocery, a small store in a home, was up the street from where my grandparents lived, on Corliss Avenue in Seattle. In case you think Max is too young for a paper route, during the war, my dad, at age ten, carried the *Seattle Daily Times* on three routes, every single day after school, arriving home long after dark. And, as it has for some eighty years, the Seattle fishing fleet receives a blessing each March, a tradition begun by the Reverend O. L. Haavik in 1929.

Most important, Duke, Missy, Pepper, Skipper, Big Boy, and Bunkie were real war dogs. A memorial in their honor stands on the island of Guam, thanks to the efforts of Captain William W. Putney, DVM, USMC. He wrote about his service as the vet for the 3rd War Dog Platoon in the moving book *Always Faithful*. That's where I read about Pfc. Marvin Corff, whose name I borrowed for this book. I wish I could have met Captain Putney and Pfc. Corff. Semper Fi, gentlemen!

I work hard to make sure that what I write is factual. But sometimes a story requires veering from the actual timing of events. One example of this is that Duke would have been at Camp Lejeune in 1943, not 1944, for his training.

The other thing to remember is that the people in this story are made up; they exist only on these pages.

And, of course, in this writer's heart.

ACKNOWLEDGMENTS

My name gets to appear on the front cover of this book, but I owe a huge debt of gratitude to so many people, including Ann Whitford Paul, who shared recipes from her copy of *Grandma's Wartime Kitchen*; Steve Remington, of the American Society of Aviation Artists, who helped with spotter model questions; and John at Old Time Radio Catalog (otrcat.com), as well as Jim Ramsburg, both Hop Harrigan experts. Thank you, Dad, for answering my nine million questions about being a kid during WWII. Finally, I am grateful to Myrtle Bruland for sharing information about Palmer Bruland's POW experiences in Stalag Luft 1, and to the many POWs who shared their stories in memoirs such as *A Fighter Pilot in Buchenwald* (Joseph F. Moser as told by Gerald R. Baron); *Hell Above and Hell Below* (Richard H. Lewis as told to William R. Larson); and *Zemke's Stalag* (Hubert Zemke as told to Roger A. Freeman). Hobie's dad's words in Chapter Sixteen were taken from a real Stalag Luft 1 POW's first postcard home.

I found treasure in *Dear Poppa: The World War II Berman Family Letters*, compiled by Ruth Berman, edited by Judy Barrett Litoff, as well as in *A War-Time Handbook for Young Americans*, by Munro Leaf.

The memorable stories of this country's brave four-legged soldiers were lovingly documented in *Always Faithful*, by Captain William W. Putney; *Dogs At War*, by Clayton G. Going; and *History of Dogs for Defense*, by Fairfax Downey. Special thanks to Roland "Mike" Jankelson for sharing his memories of donating his dog, Laddie, to Dogs for Defense.

None of my books would get off the ground without the assistance of the amazing librarians at Seattle Public Library, King County Library, and all of their colleagues around the country.

I can't write a word without Mary Nethery, who manages to make sure my novels actually have plots. I'd be pulling espresso shots if not for the guidance of Jill Grinberg, agent extraordinaire. And I would never, ever have found the heart of Hobie's story without Lisa Sandell, who is a real sweetheart but drives a tough bargain when it comes to making a really good book. And, thank you, Whitney Lyle, for this book's stunning design. These acknowledgments would not be complete without a nod to the adorable Lily Bess and her beach buddy Esme, as well as to Neil, who never wanted a dog but is now as crazy about Winston as I am.

ABOUT THE AUTHOR

Kirby Larson is the acclaimed author of the 2007 Newbery Honor book *Hattie Big Sky*; its sequel, *Hattie Ever After*; *The Friendship Doll*; and *Dear America: The Fences Between Us*. She has also cowritten two award-winning picture books about dogs: *Two Bobbies: A True Story of Hurricane Katrina, Friendship, and Survival*, and *Nubs: The True Story of a Mutt, a Marine & a Miracle*. She lives in Washington State with her husband and Winston the Wonder Dog.